The
Dreamseller:
THE REVOLUTION

Also by Augusto Cury

The Dreamseller: The Calling

The Dreamseller:
THE REVOLUTION

A NOVEL

AUGUSTO CURY

ATRIA PAPERBACK

New York   Toronto   London   Sydney   New Delhi

ATRIA PAPERBACK

A Division of Simon & Schuster, Inc.
1230 Avenue of the Americas
New York, NY 10020

Originally published in Brazil in 2009 in Portuguese by Instituto Academia de Inteligência Ltda. as *O Vendedor de Sonhos e a Revolução dos Anônimos*.

Published by arrangement with Instituto Academia de Inteligência Ltda.

First Atria Paperback edition September 2012

ATRIA PAPERBACK and colophon are trademarks of Simon & Schuster, Inc.

For information about special discounts for bulk purchases, please contact Simon & Schuster Special Sales at 1-866-506-1949 or business@simonandschuster.com.

The Simon & Schuster Speakers Bureau can bring authors to your live event. For more information or to book an event, contact the Simon & Schuster Speakers Bureau at 1-866-248-3049 or visit our website at www.simonspeakers.com.

Manufactured in the United States of America

10   9   8   7   6   5   4   3   2   1

The Library of Congress Cataloging-in-Publication Data is available.

ISBN 978-1-4391-9605-2
ISBN 978-1-4391-9607-6 (ebook)

To all the anonymous people in society who understand that existence is a great contract with risk. And to those who read the clauses of that contract that drama and comedy, loss and gain, desert and oasis, calm and stress are privileges that belong to the living.

Contents

Contents

Preface

THE DREAMSELLER IS A SAGA TOLD IN SEVERAL VOLUMES with the same characters. In this saga, drama and comedy, pain and laughter, sanity and madness permeate the texts and roil the story. Though there is a sequence, each book can be read separately. I was not expecting the first book, *The Dreamseller: The Calling*, to have such explosive success overseas, especially because it is intensely critical of the social system and denounces modern societies as having become huge mental institutions in which being sick is normal.

The Calling introduces a mysterious character—the dreamseller, whose origin and history are unknown and who "calls" the wanderers to follow him on a risky journey to reflect upon and denounce the madness of the social system. The disciples are wild, eccentric, complex and confused. The dreamseller prods his listeners to search the most important place of all, a place that even kings have rarely found: the inner reaches of the human soul.

In the second book, *The Revolution,* the dreamseller continues to turn society upside down. His "crazy" disciples, among whom Bartholomew and Barnabas stand out, spread their wings, revealing a surprising creativity and causing endless and unexpected adventures. They provoke everything and everyone, including the dreamseller himself. This novel demonstrates that societies are made up of anonymous heroes.

Among the anonymous are the depressed, who confront their emotions with dignity; the anxious, who dream of calmer days; cancer patients, who fight for life and make each day an eternal moment; parents, who exhaust body and mind to support and educate their children; teachers, who, for meager salaries and without praise from society, move the world by teaching critical thinking to their students; students, who quixotically believe they can change history, unaware that they live in an unbending social system hardly sympathetic to new ideas; workers in offices and firms, who go unnoticed unless they cause a scene but who have uplifting stories. All of them are in some way dreamsellers—although they also sell nightmares.

Every human being is a vault of secrets. Exploring them, spending time with them is a privilege. As a psychiatrist, psychotherapist and author of a theory that studies the intriguing world of complex thinking, I have learned a great deal from each of those anonymous individuals. I've discovered a treasure buried in their minds. I feel small next to many of them.

The Dreamseller: The Revolution, by emphasizing these anonymous figures, reflects the amazing complexity of our history, which is written with tears and joy, calm and anxiety, sanity and madness.

CHAPTER 1

A Controversial and Surprising Man

WE WERE LIVING IN A TIME WHEN PEOPLE, DEVOID OF creativity and caught in a web of sameness, were overly predictable. Actors and actresses, show business personalities, politicians, religious leaders, executives of large corporations— all were tiring, boring and often insufferable. They were repetitious in their worn-out jargon. They neither appealed to emotion nor inspired the intellect. They needed a marketing strategy and a media makeover to repackage them and render them interesting. Even young people no longer had any enthusiasm for their idols.

Suddenly, as we rode the waves of tedium, a man appeared, breaking the imprisonment of routine. He turned our minds upside down, or at least my mind and the minds of those closest to him. He became the greatest sociological phenomenon of our time. Though he shunned the attention of the media, it was all but impossible to remain indifferent to his thoughts.

Without revealing his identity, he declared himself a seller of dreams and, inviting others to join him, soon blew like a hurricane into the heart of the great city. He was an enigmatic stranger followed by strangers. And he made demands:

"Whoever would follow me must first recognize his madness and face his stupidity." And he proclaimed to passersby,

"Happy are those who are transparent, for theirs is the king-dom of mental health and wisdom. Unhappy are those who hide their sickness behind their schooling, money or social standing, for theirs is the kingdom of insanity. But let's be hon-est. We are all experts at hiding. We squeeze into the tiniest of holes to hide, even under the banner of sincerity."

The man rocked society, astounding those who heard him. Wherever he went, he caused a ruckus. He lived beneath bridges and overpasses or in homeless shelters. Never in our time had someone so unassuming had such impact. A pauper without health insurance, welfare or money for his meals, he had the courage to say:

"I ask not that you be wanderers like me. My dream is that you will be wanderers in your own right, that you make your way through territories few intellectuals dare to explore. Fol-low no map or compass. Search for yourselves, lose yourselves. Make each day a new chapter, every twist in the road a new story."

He criticized modern man, who lived like a machine, never pondering what it meant to be a thinking being or reflecting on the mysteries of existence. Mankind walked in the shallows of existence and intellect. Some protested, "Who is this audacious invader of our private lives? What insane asylum did he escape from?" Others discovered that they had no time for what was essential, especially for themselves.

Only a small group of friends slept where he slept and lived where he lived. I was one of them. Those who crossed his path didn't know if what they were seeing was real or imagined.

His origins were unknown even to his disciples. When asked about his identity, he would repeat, "I'm a wanderer moving on the path of time, looking for himself."

He was destitute but had what millionaires lacked. His

home was expansive: sometimes park benches, sometimes the steps of a building or the shade of a tree. His gardens extended throughout the city. He contemplated them as if they were the Hanging Gardens of Babylon, cultivated only to enchant his eyes. Of every flower, he made a poem, of every leaf a dart to plunge into the wellsprings of sensibility, of every weathered tree trunk a moment to soar on the wings of imagination.

"Dawns do not go unappreciated. Sunsets do not go unnoticed but invite me to repose and to think about my folly," the dreamseller would say. He behaved unlike anyone we'd ever met. While others loved to glorify themselves, he enjoyed reflecting on his smallness.

One morning, after barely sleeping under a highway overpass, he stretched, took several deep breaths, and drank in the morning sunlight. After reflection, he went to the center of a nearby university campus and shouted to the students:

"We are free to come and go but not to think. Our thoughts and choices are restricted to the confines of our brains. How can we be free if we cover our bodies with clothing but our minds are stark naked? How can we be free if we contaminate the present with the future, if we steal from the present our inalienable right to drink from the fountain of tranquillity?"

On one occasion, three psychiatrists passing by heard one of his speeches. One of them was taken with the ragged stranger, but the other two said, "That man is a danger to society. He should be locked up."

Reading their lips, he replied, "Don't worry, my friends, I'm already locked up. Just look around at this grand and beautiful mental hospital."

In modern societies, child labor was outlawed, but the dreamseller said that those same nations committed a crime against children by encumbering their minds with mass consumption, allowing them to grow up too fast, and overloading them with activities.

"Our children are spared the horrors of war; they don't see houses destroyed or mutilated bodies, but their imagination is obliterated, their capacity for play inhibited, their imagination kidnapped by unnecessary trinkets. Isn't that its own form of horror?" he said. "There's a reason that depression and other emotional disturbances among children and adolescents have increased so much." He said this with tears in his eyes. His own children had perished in a tragic accident, but at the time, we knew nothing about the details of his mysterious past.

Once, at the end of classes, he "invaded" a private elementary school whose pupils were the children of upper-middle- and upper-class parents. Granite floors, marble columns, stained-glass windows, air-conditioned classrooms. Every pupil had a personal computer. The only problem was that the children were restless, found no delight in learning and were not developing critical thinking. To them, school and the educational environment were almost unbearable. As soon as they heard the bell, they would dash out as if released from prison.

Their parents, when they came for them, didn't have a minute to spare. They would scold their children if they were late. The dreamseller slipped past security, put on a clown nose and began running, jumping, dancing in the patio. When they saw this crazy man, many of the nine- and ten-year-olds forgot they were on their way out and went over to watch him.

Opening his arms like an airplane, he pretended to fly to a small garden. There, he imitated a toad, a cricket and a rattlesnake. Then he performed magic tricks. He produced a flower from his sleeve and a bunny from his jacket. And after a few minutes of amusement he told the attentive children:

"Behold the greatest magic of all." And he took a seed from

his pocket. "If you were a seed, what kind of tree would you like to grow into?" He asked them to close their eyes and imagine the tree they would be. Each child imagined a different tree, from the diameter of the trunk, the shape of the crown and the size of the branches, to the most diverse types of leaves and flowers.

Several parents were desperately looking for their children. They had never been ten minutes late leaving class. Some feared they had been kidnapped. The teachers also went looking for them. When they found the dreamseller in the garden, they were impressed by how quiet the children were, especially at that time of day. They saw the ragged man and realized that the person stirring up the school was the same stranger who was inciting the city.

Then he told the children, "A life without dreams is a seed without soil, a plant without nourishment. Dreams don't determine the kind of tree you'll be, but they give you strength to understand there's no growth without storms, times of difficulty and misunderstanding. Play more, smile more, imagine more. Cover yourselves in the dirt of your dreams. Without dirt, a seed can't germinate." And he scooped up some of the clay beside him and smeared it on his face.

Amazed, several of the children also stuck their hands in the clay and dirtied their faces. Some stained their clothes. They would never forget that day, even when they were old. However, when their parents arrived and saw their children dirty and being taught by a ratty-looking stranger, they were horrified. "Get that maniac away from our children!" some said.

"We pay a fortune in tuition and the school doesn't offer the least bit of security. It's an outrage!" others shouted.

They called security, who roughly tossed the dreamseller out of the school in front of the children. Juliana, a nine-year-old with the most dirt on her face, ran to him and shouted, "Stop, stop!"

Surprised, the guards stopped. Juliana handed the dreamseller a flower and said, "I'd like to be a grapevine."

"Why, my child?"

"It's not pretty or strong like you. But anyone can reach its fruit."

"You will be a great seller of dreams," the dreamseller said.

Some of the teachers asked the security guards to go easy on the man. As he left, some applauded. Turning to them, he said:

"A society that encourages those who punish over those who educate will always be sick. I would not bow to the famous or the great leaders of our society, but I bow down to the educators."

And he bowed before the open-mouthed teachers.

It was not easy to accompany that mysterious man. He spoke in places where you were supposed to keep quiet, danced in places where you were supposed to sit still. He was unpredictable. Sometimes he would distance himself from his disciples to avoid involving them in the tumult he caused.

One of the things that most disheartened him was how unhappy people seemed to be in the digital age, something unforeseen by Freud. He would often say:

"We are morbid, weary and perpetually discontent. Yet the entertainment industry is at its peak, and the sale of depression medication has gone through the roof. Doesn't that bother you, ladies and gentlemen?"

People did seem troubled. Some by his words, others by the man himself.

"We watch sitcoms every night, but where are our smiles the next morning? We have pleasures the Greeks never dreamed of, but where is the enduring joy? And the patience?"

The dreamseller didn't worry about whether he was lauded or ridiculed. He was concerned only with being faithful to what he believed. To him, life was far too short to be lived in a false, futile, mediocre way. One of the manifestations of mediocrity that he fought against most fiercely was the cult of celebrity.

"Those who live outside the media spotlight, the anonymous toilers who struggle to survive, the health professionals who save lives, the assembly line workers, the trash collectors, those are the true stars in society. But just as it trivializes these heroes, the system handpicks its celebrities. A society that promotes celebrities is emotionally stunted and sick."

To some, the dreamseller was the craziest of crazies. To others, a thinker of unprecedented daring. And some saw him as a man who had been great and fallen from his throne. To me, he was stimulating, extraordinary, controversial. His speeches cut like razors, his ideas were enthralling. He was both loved and hated like no other.

I had been a prideful intellectual and egotistical professor of sociology who always felt the need to be praised and to control my students. For six months, I had been following this man with the long, unruly hair and untrimmed beard, this man who wore clothes so wrinkled and torn, you'd never even find them at a secondhand store.

But this man was so captivating that groups of teenagers would wake up at sunrise on Saturdays and Sundays to seek him out. They wanted to find out what kind of uproar he and his disciples would get into. Some of his disciples seemed so crazy that their illnesses couldn't even be found in psychology textbooks. And, to be honest, there were times when I felt like running away and abandoning our group. But something about his mission fascinated me.

The dreamseller wasn't balanced like a Christian monk, serene like a Buddhist monk, and he was much less deliberate than a philosopher from Greece's Golden Age. Sometimes he led us to calm waters, other times into the eye of the storm. When people praised him, he might say, "Careful, I'm not normal. Some think I'm mentally ill. Following me is risky."

He could spend hours talking to a blind man and say that of the two, the blind man could see more than he. Young people wanted to discuss their crises and passions. He might interrupt a brilliant speech and abruptly leave a crowd if he spotted an elderly man having trouble walking. He would accompany his halting steps for blocks on end and listen with delight to the conversation.

I asked myself what kind of man was this who expended energy on things we considered irrelevant. He was capable of creating poetry from a glass of water and drinking it in a way we never did. Raising the glass, he said:

"O, water that quenches my thirst, one day I will disintegrate in a tomb, and you, in a thousand particles, will return to the bed of the sea. But you will weep with longing for humanity. Released, you will evaporate, travel to distant places and, like tears, once again fall to refresh other people."

Free of the neurotic need for power, he did not worry about his image. He lived without glamour, ostentation or self-promotion. When we walked with him, the hundred billion neurons that make up our brains were in a constant state of alert. Living with this man meant laying bare our foolishness, revealing our madness.

This man rescued me when I was on the verge of suicide. Afterward, he might have gone on his way and I mine, perhaps never to meet again. But what he said to keep me from killing myself floored me. For the very first time, I bowed before another man's wisdom. I was ready to end my life, to punctuate my existence with a period when he made me a disturbing offer:

"I want to sell you a comma."

"A comma?" I asked.

"Yes, a comma, so you can pause, then go on writing your life, for a man without a comma is a man without a history."

That was the moment I realized I had used periods instead of commas throughout my life. If someone frustrated me, I would eliminate him, putting a period to our relationship. Someone injured me? I would erase him. If I encountered an obstacle? I would change directions. If my plan had problems? I would replace it. If I suffered a loss? I would turn my back.

As a professor, I learned from the books of others but didn't know how to write the book of my existence. I considered myself an angel and those who frustrated me, demons, without ever acknowledging that I had been the one who alienated my wife, my only child, my friends and my students.

Whoever eliminates everyone around him will one day decide to eliminate himself. And that day had arrived. But luckily, I had found the dreamseller and come to understand that frustrations, disappointments, betrayals, abuse and conflict are all part of life. And commas are essential.

I lived comfortably in my small apartment on a professor's meager salary. Then I, a socialist who had always criticized the bourgeoisie and sang the praises of society's poor, came to experience the pain of poverty in my own life.

I became a follower of a seller of ideas who had nothing. Marx, a theoretical thinker who never knew what it meant to be a proletarian, would have been perplexed by this man. When I began following the dreamseller, I realized Marx was a hypocrite who defended something he didn't know. Therefore I left behind the frontiers of theory to become a wanderer, a small seller of commas to help people free their minds, rewrite their history and develop critical thinking.

Being mocked, jeered, branded a lunatic, an impostor—

these were the smallest risks in joining the group. The worst? Being beaten, arrested, labeled a rioter, kidnapper and a terrorist. Selling dreams in a society that has stopped dreaming came at a very high cost.

But nothing was more exciting. Those who joined our group knew nothing of boredom, anguish or depression. We did, however, run unforeseeable risks.

CHAPTER 2

Deliver Me from These Disciples!

FOLLOWING THE DREAMSELLER DOESN'T SEEM SUITED FOR someone who had been applauded in universities and respected by his fellow professors.

Some of my old colleagues from the university thought I'd lost my mind. I discovered that just as cattle are marked with a hot branding iron, in some sectors of the university, colleagues are branded with the flames of prejudice. I was among the worst offenders, but this time, I was the one being prejudged.

Was it insane to follow this man? Probably. But it seemed a more lucid insanity than living the life of "normals" who spend hours a day in front of their televisions, waiting for death, without ever venturing forth and fighting for a dream. An insanity saner than spending your days clutching a cell phone, in touch with the world but out of touch with yourself. An insanity more fertile than those who defend their theses in order to avoid controversy, not knowing that great ideas are born of the soil of risk and humiliation. As thesis adviser, I avoided controversy—and suffocated thinkers.

What I have been doing since is the most fantastic sociological experiment in recent times. Naturally, there are side effects to this journey, and they have nothing to do with prejudice or the hardship of following a fearless, bold and critical man.

They're due mainly to the team of disciples he has invited to follow him. They drive me crazy, especially Bartholomew and Barnabas.

Bartholomew is a recovering alcoholic. Still, his greatest problem isn't alcoholism but compulsive speech syndrome—CSS. He's hooked on always offering his two cents. He likes to philosophize but trips over his words. His nickname says it all: "Honeymouth." His mouth is bigger than his brain. Unlike the dreamseller, he's brash, but I have to admit that he has a contagious happiness, an enviable sense of humor.

Barnabas is also a recovering alcoholic and was a longtime boozing companion of Bartholomew's. Both are experts at putting their foot in their mouth. Barnabas is addicted both to alcohol and to giving political speeches, thus his nickname, "The Mayor." Whenever he sees a gathering of people, his brain goes into a trance, he swells his chest, modulates his voice, and tries to persuade people to vote for him—for what office, no one knows. Unlike the dreamseller, he loves applause and recognition. Honeymouth is thin, lanky. The Mayor is an obese, good-natured slob and always has something hidden in his jacket to chew on. Honeymouth is a street philosopher; the Mayor, a street politician.

To them, intellectuals like me are imbeciles. They love to provoke me. Despite being irreligious, I sometimes pray, "God, deliver me from these disciples!" To make things worse, Bartholomew and Barnabas compete with each other like children. Besides trying my patience, they diminish the dreamseller's philosophical depth. Whenever they're around, drama turns to comedy.

Even when they have no problems, they find a way to create some. And the worst part is they drag in everyone around them, including the dreamseller. Frankly, to this day I can't understand why he chose them. I thought he should have chosen cultured, experienced, well-behaved individuals such as executives, psychologists, teachers or doctors. But he preferred those rabble-rousers.

Once, in the middle of a discussion, the dreamseller stated poetically a truth about human existence that applies directly to every mortal, rich or poor: "Existence is cyclical. No applause lasts forever and no jeers are eternal."

That thought led me to reflect on the great men in history. Jesus Christ was loved by many but was betrayed by his closest friends. Julius Caesar's closest friends, Brutus and Cassius, betrayed and assassinated him. Napoleon rose and fell like few others. Lincoln, Kennedy, Martin Luther King all had short lives.

Bartholomew couldn't keep quiet, and looking to stand out from the crowd, he disagreed with the dreamseller.

"Boss, I'm afraid your theory doesn't apply to me." he said. "My life isn't cyclical. I've been down for years. I'm made fun of, cursed, called a bum, a shameless good-for-nothing. I go from one mess to another."

Barnabas, the Mayor, upon hearing Bartholomew hold the crowd's attention, couldn't resist jumping in like a stumping politician.

"Distinguished dreamseller, ladies and gentlemen, if Honeymouth has been living years of misery, I must declare that I have lived a miserable life as long as I can remember. I'm lost in the woods without a compass, a cell phone, a credit card or money." He raised his voice and added, "But, I trust the dreamseller's words that life is cyclical and the day will come when I will be called upon by the people. For in this city there are only two types of voters: those who vote for me and those who haven't met me." This pair was so shameless that they competed not only to be the best but also to be the worst. I could only conclude the dreamseller had called them to follow him because he pitied them.

Once, he commented to his circle of friends:

"I leaped among the mountaintops like a ram, never imagining I could fall. But the day came when I stumbled through the hostile valleys of anguish, in a place where few mental health specialists have gone. That's when I discovered that I knew nothing about myself. I learned I was a stranger in my own home, unknown even to myself."

Astonished by that discovery and shaken by his unfathomable losses, he isolated himself on an island for more than three years. Time stopped. Everything and nothing became one and the same. Profoundly depressed although his table overflowed with food, he had an appetite only for knowledge.

"I would consume books day and night, sitting or standing, walking or running. I devoured books on philosophy, neuroscience, history, sociology, psychology, theology. Books became my passport to travel the world of the mind."

After this process, he pulled himself together and returned to society. But, no longer the same man, he didn't look upon life as he had before. He did not become a hero or a messiah, but a human being conscious of his imperfections, aware of his own madness and the madness of the world around him. He did not want to change the world but to shout about other paths. Selling dreams became his reason for being.

Many questions still torment me when I think about his story. What does he want from us? Why is he bent on challenging others' minds? Is he running away from something? Had he really been such an important figure? How can someone who was once highly respected let himself be labeled an impostor, a psychotic, a rebel? Who was he?

After telling us a little bit about his past, he fell silent. He spoke no more about it. We didn't know whether he was being figurative or if everything he said was true. But what worried us most is that he started risking his life.

We couldn't imagine who would want to hurt—much less assassinate—a man who radiated such gentleness and generosity. Concerned about the safety of his friends, he tried to distance himself from us. But we insisted on staying.

"Boss, if you need a man to protect you, here I am!" Bartholomew said. "Nobody close to me has ever died. Well, I mean, they've been beaten, battered, pummeled, but not killed."

In a serious tone, the Mayor declared his loyalty to the dreamseller: "With me at your side, you'll be safe from all dangers, including the ones Honeymouth causes."

I couldn't take it. He was talking his head off and not paying attention to the dreamseller's words.

I felt like slapping him. But we were dealing with protecting the dreamseller.

Dimas, the con man in our group, decided to show his loyalty, even though no purse or wallet was ever safe around him.

"Dreamseller, safety is my middle name. You can count on me."

Dimas was in recovery, but he was still a kleptomaniac; when certain objects came into sight, they would trigger a compulsive attempt to possess them.

At that moment, Edson, the group's religious voice, saw his favorite pen in Dimas's pocket. "Hey, that's my pen," he said.

Without missing a beat, the cunning Dimas told him, "I know. I was taking care of it for you." And he returned it.

Edson thought he had supernatural gifts and was always trying to perform miracles. After getting his pen back, he told the dreamseller:

"My prayers will protect you."

After weighing the band of misfits around the dreamseller,

I wondered whether he wouldn't be safer surrounded by his enemies. We were the most unconventional family ever. The dreamseller trained us to be patient and calm, but those virtues were luxuries to us. We broke all the sociological rules.

How long would we follow him? We didn't know. What surprises and setbacks awaited us? We couldn't guess. Would we sell dreams or worsen an already tottering society? Everything was tinged with doubt. The future was the mother of uncertainty.

CHAPTER 3

A Market of Crazies

T HE DREAMSELLER NEVER SERVED UP HIS IDEAS ON A platter. He made us enter the "kitchen" of our intellects and fend for ourselves. To him, whoever can't fend for himself doesn't know how to think.

Once, we were in the beautiful but busy courtyard of the federal courthouse. There was a huge monument to independence, with a cast-iron horse nine feet high, atop an enormous thirty-foot concrete pillar. Mounted on the animal was a soldier, also iron, holding a sword. He seemed to be shouting, rallying his troops to battle. As he passed the monument, the dreamseller pointed to the soldier and said:

"Behold a reflection of how mankind has always believed more in arms than in ideas. But who are the strong ones—those who use weapons or those who use ideas?"

Honeymouth had no doubts. "Those who use cannons, machine guns, rockets."

"But isn't it ideas that build the weapons, Bartholomew?" the dreamseller replied, hoping to correct him.

"Yes."

Then the dreamseller said, "If ideas are strong enough to build weapons, they should be strong enough to find solutions to avoid our having to use them. But, once built, weapons turn us against ideas. The creature destroys the creator."

We went on walking. The country's legal eagles passed through the courtyard. Lawyers, judges, prosecutors, public defenders, justice officials—all wearing impeccable suits that contrasted with our rags, especially the dreamseller's. He was wearing a threadbare and wrinkled coat with a large tear on its left side, ventilating his back.

Watching the others rush by, he began inviting them to a forum on the human mind. He bombarded them with questions as they passed.

"Doesn't the ability to formulate thoughts enchant you, ladies and gentlemen? How we penetrate the immense area of the cerebral cortex, millions of times more complex than the districts of this great city, and succeed in finding the pieces that comprise even the poorest of thoughts? Doesn't that astound you? Isn't the most despicable of human beings, by possessing this capability, a genius, even if he fails in school or has a below-average IQ? How do we penetrate the unfathomable labyrinths of the mind and, amid billions of options, pull verbs from our mental files and conjugate them without knowing beforehand where they're found and what tense we'll use? Doesn't this feat dazzle you? We may act different from one another, but the phenomena that make us *Homo sapiens* are exactly the same, whether we're judges or prisoners, prosecutors or criminals."

This bombardment of queries perplexed me. I wondered: Where did he get his ability to ask questions and draw these conclusions? His questions were so complex that they knotted the minds of his disciples.

The jurists passing through the courtyard were disturbed by the avalanche of questions. They used their brains all the time, but they never thought about thinking. One said, "Who is that madman?" Another, more thoughtful, asked, "What university does this thinker come from?" And still others wondered, "Is this some kind of street theater?" The dreamseller's questioning penetrated the cerebral circuits of those men, hard workers who never had time to reflect on the mental phenomena behind thought, or on human anguish and conflicts. Only a few stopped.

The Mayor, whispering in our ears, came out with this piece of nonsense: "Once I've had a few, I know the answers to all those questions," the Mayor joked.

Although others ignored him, the dreamseller went on: "I have something extremely dear to sell you, ladies and gentlemen. Come closer! Lend me your ears."

Some of them stopped to look at the stranger, wondering what he was selling. His most befuddled disciple broke the silence.

"I'll take one, dreamseller! I'll pay for it! It's mine!" Bartholomew said, without actually knowing what the dreamseller was selling.

But his big mouth actually started a bidding war. And seeing Honeymouth gaining attention, the Mayor shouted louder, "No, it's mine. I'll pay more! Two thousand."

Passersby were annoyed with the noisy pair. People asked, "Buy what?" "How much does it cost?"

Drawn in by an eccentric selling an invisible product and two lunatics willing to spend everything they had to buy it, people finally stopped to watch the show.

"I'll pay a million!" Honeymouth said.

Barnabas bid louder. "I'll pay a billion!"

Watching these two clowns, I, the first to be called by the dreamseller as a disciple, wanted to find a hole to crawl into. Once again they were diminishing the dreamseller's ideas. The somber courtyard became like Babylon: No one understood anyone else.

And then, I had a disturbing thought: "Could it be that the dreamseller chose Bartholomew and Barnabas to serve as mirrors so people like me could see their own insanity?"

As I struggled with these thoughts, my reasoning expanded. I began to think these loons were authentic, and I was the one pretending. They said whatever came to mind, while I hid my real intentions. They smiled without fear and cried without regret. No one ever learned about my emotional troubles until they exploded.

I began to realize that society, and later the university, had taught me to gloss over my emotions. Actors work in theaters, intellectuals in the arenas of knowledge, but down deep we're all masters of disguise.

The Mayor, still trying to win this mythical auction, upped the bid. But Bartholomew, who never conceded defeat, especially to the Mayor, shouted, "I'll give a trillion!"

The Mayor filled his lungs to make an even higher bid, but since he didn't know the word "quadrillion," he appealed to the dreamseller. "Noble Master, Honeymouth is the biggest deadbeat in the world. He buys, but he doesn't pay."

"That's a lie, ladies and gentlemen," said Honeymouth. Turning to the lawyers witnessing the scene in astonishment, he asked, "Who wants the privilege of being my lawyer to sue this man for slander?" No one raised his hand. However, more than a few burst into laughter. It had been a long time since they felt relaxed.

I was shaking with rage. We had lost the philosophical atmosphere the dreamseller had created. Peter denied Christ three times. Silently, I have been denying the dreamseller daily. It's hard for me to acknowledge that I'm part of this group of troublemakers.

Just when I thought the dreamseller was disappointed with his disciples, I saw his calm, smiling expression. The breeze spread his hair softly onto the right side of his face. The wind stirred the leaves on the trees.

It was a circus and a classroom, all at once. He didn't care at all about the humiliation. For him, jeers and applause were one and the same. He didn't let either get to him. I dreamed of such freedom, but I was a prisoner of my mental dungeon.

CHAPTER 4

What Is Truly Dear

INSPIRED, THE DREAMSELLER GAZED ACROSS THE ALMOST fifty people gathered in the courtyard, then turned to his two bungling disciples and gave them a great lesson. I was fascinated.

"Barnabas, Bartholomew and friends. Everything that can be sold is cheap; even if it costs a billion dollars, there's someone with the money to buy it. Only that which can't be sold is expensive," he stated. "Money buys tranquilizers, but not the ability to relax. It buys hangers-on, but not the shoulder of a friend. It buys jewels, but not a woman's love. It buys a painting, but not the ability to contemplate one. It buys insurance, but not the capacity for protecting our emotions."

He breathed deeply before continuing: "Money buys information, but not self-awareness. It buys glasses, but not the ability to see unexpressed feelings. It buys a manual with rules for raising our children, but not a manual for life."

Hearing the dreamseller's simple yet cutting words, I remembered my son John Marcus. And how I had gone so wrong with my boy. Only now did I understand that I had never given him what can't be sold. I criticized, confronted, punished and put limits on him. I was nothing but a soulless manual of rules and ethics. I abused him emotionally. I corrected him in front of his peers.

I never once gave him a shoulder to cry on. Never said that his father also had fears, had made mistakes and countless times was inconsistent. The dreamseller's first rule: to recognize your madness and your stupidity. I didn't recognize them. I was more machine than teacher, trying to shape thinkers. I considered myself a god educating a human being.

From a sociological point of view, I knew that men who have committed history's greatest atrocities were those who acted like gods. They killed, injured and conquered, never knowing their own frailties, as if they were immortal. We reproduce the attitudes of such atrocious men in the least expected places—in our living rooms, classrooms, offices, courts.

I looked around and saw illustrious judges and attorneys, their eyes swimming with tears. They were like me, cultured but vulnerable; gigantic but small; eloquent when speaking of the outside world but reluctant to speak about themselves with their loved ones.

Some of the attorneys around us were extremely rich, but had only bought what was cheap in life. They were never really millionaires. While the dreamseller had the attorneys' heads in the clouds, Bartholomew appeared to bring them back to earth. He yelled to Barnabas:

"I'm richer than people loaded with dough. I don't buy jewels, but women love me. I don't buy paintings, but I contemplate the sky. I don't have groupies, but I have an interesting set of friends." And to jerk our chain, he added, "Hey, Julio Cesar, Edson and Dimas snore like goats but I still don't need pills to sleep."

The Mayor wasn't about to be outdone. Seeing the captive audience, he tried to win it over by using a big word he didn't understand.

"I am richer than you, Mr. Bigmouth. I'm a very *turpitudinous* person." He didn't know that "turpitudinous" meant shameful, wicked, depraved. Actually, he didn't realize how right he was. And he continued, "Ah, cherished society! If you but knew who I am you would love me."

The lawyers bursted out laughing. When the laughter died down, the dreamseller elaborated a thought I'd never had. "When we leave the womb of our mother and enter the womb of society, we cry. When we leave the womb of society and enter the womb of our eternal graves, others cry for us. Coming into life and leaving it, tears punctuate our story. Why, ladies and gentlemen?"

I wondered how he managed to think straight in this commotion. His disciples were disruptive, traffic on the streets was snarled, but as if removed from all of it, he displayed a startling ability to construct unusual ideas.

The dreamseller asked questions we had forgotten how to ask. I didn't know the answer to his question. Seeing our silence, he prodded us:

"Whoever isn't amazed by the phenomenon of existence is like a child who lives without having the slightest awareness of life."

Living has become a banal phenomenon, no longer amazing. Many spent a dozen or more years in school without being even minimally conscious of their role as human beings. The dreamseller resumed his questioning and redirected it to the lawyers:

"Why, ladies and gentlemen of the legal profession, do we cry when we leave the maternal womb and others shed tears when we leave the social womb for the cold womb of a grave?"

I was hoping Bartholomew and Barnabas wouldn't open their mouths this time and spoil the intellectual journey. But this time it was young Solomon who spoke up.

Solomon is a sensitive, intelligent disciple who is also obsessive and a hypochondriac. He improved alongside the dreamseller but frequently suffered relapses. If the day was sunny, he feared he'd suffer heatstroke; if it rained, he feared he'd catch a cold. And his most irresistible obsession was sticking his finger into any hole he saw.

"Tears in this life are due to cancer, encephalitis, pancreatitis, duodenitis, heart attacks, aneurisms, cerebrovascular accidents . . ." And he went on to list more than a dozen other diseases we had never heard of.

The audience looked at each other as he rambled on. I furrowed my brow, Bartholomew and Barnabas scratched their heads. The dreamseller thanked the young man for his participation. To him, debate was as important as finding an answer.

"Well, done, Solomon. But I'm going to take a different approach. The tears at the beginning and the end of life reveal that existence is the greatest of all spectacles, marked by countless emotions. Drama and comedy. Gentle breezes and heavy storms. Health and sickness. All are privileges of the living. From young children to the elderly, from Westerners to Asians, all of us experience success and defeat, fidelity and betrayal, relief and pain to some degree."

I pondered his words. I had never considered pain and failure a privilege, but indeed only the living can experience them. I had bombarded my students with information but never prepared them for the miracle of existence. I educated the young with college degrees but I left them unprepared to deal with loss, adversity, scorn, betrayal, frustration.

The dreamseller didn't want us to be masochists and seek out suffering. Just the opposite. But neither did he want us to be naïve. He believed that whoever denies or flees from pain only increases it. Facing one's losses fearfully merely adds fuel to his anguish, turning our spectacle of an existence into a limited script. I had the impression that he had learned this lesson from his own past. He seemed to suggest that when he had suc-

cumbed to his emotional demons, he had tried to ignore them
and only succeeded in making them stronger. At the same time,
I had the feeling, right or wrong, that he wanted not only to
sell dreams to the lawyers but also to prepare his disciples for
the tumult we would face at his side. I felt afraid and forgot for
a few moments what he had just taught us. It's so hard to learn
the language of emotion.

While I was meditating on his words, Bartholomew intervened again, and this time he touched everyone, including me.
He fearlessly told his story, speaking in a voice filled with emotion:

"Master, when I was expelled from my mother's womb and
entered the womb of society, I shed lots of tears. My father was
an alcoholic and often beat me. He died when I was seven. My
mother left me at an orphanage. She told me she had cancer
and couldn't take care of me. Three or four years earlier, she
had taken my only brother to an orphanage, or to a foster family, I'm not sure. They told me my mother died, but they never
told me about her funeral. I never had a chance to grieve. I
shed tears and more tears crying for her and for my brother,
but no one heard me. I was adopted for a short time, but my
adoptive parents couldn't stand me and left me at another orphanage. I grew up without a family. I grew up alone, deeply
alone. I was battered in the womb of society," he said, with a
sensitivity he had never before expressed. He didn't seem like
the Bartholomew I knew. But, in fact, this helped explain the
Honeymouth who always sought a place in society where he
could finally be seen and heard. "The only affection I received
was from my dog. I named him Terrorist. Terrorist had fleas for
company, and Terrorist was company for me."

I was very moved. The Mayor listened to Bartholomew's
tale and, wiping tears from his eyes, recounted a part of his
own existential desert.

"I understand you, my friend," he said, sadly. "I was the prettiest little plump child in the world, but my parents abandoned me on the doorstep of a skinny couple who—on top of everything else—were vegetarians. They tried to nourish this body with spinach, carrot juice and vegetables. I went to bed hungry every night. They saw eye to eye on food but not on life. They would fight every day. I was their punching bag. Whenever I cried, they would stick a carrot in my mouth. To this day I shudder when I see a carrot. As if that weren't enough, they spanked me. Finally, they put me in an orphanage at the age of six—an orphanage run by vegetarians. I was so hungry I wanted to eat an entire cow out of spite!" He paused and grew solemn. "Who would ever adopt a little boy that age—no matter how cute he was? I grew up without love or affection."

Hugging his friend, he said, "And just like you, Honeymouth, the only kisses I ever got in the orphanage were from my dog, Spook. I would fall asleep every night with Spook at my feet."

The Mayor didn't care who was starting at him or judging him. Now I understand why he always has food stashed away. He had gone hungry. I felt guilty for having criticized them. The closest onlookers teared up. A couple placed a hand on his shoulder. The dreamseller was moved. But, just as everyone was touched by their stories, the incorrigible pair inevitably reverted to their usual selves.

"Mayor, this show's way too depressing," Honeymouth said. "The only way to drown our sorrows is with a pint—or ten."

"I hear you, Honeymouth. This womb of society is too sad to endure. I think we need to go get hammered."

Professor Jurema, another of the dreamseller's disciples, an elderly former educator, was a patient and intelligent woman, just like Monica, the ex-model who was also part of the group. When the two heard the nonsense Bartholomew and Barnabas

were spouting, they both started to cough, trying to drown out
their words. I joined in. The three of us were the most level-
headed of the disciples.

But the crowd was enjoying itself. The attorneys, judges,
and prosecutors came down from the heights of existential reflection to the level of barroom humor.

Jurema grabbed her cane and hooked it around Bartholomew's neck, uttering the famous phrase, "Bartholomew,
with your mouth shut you're irreplaceable."

"Settle down, folks. I didn't mean get loaded on booze—but
on philosophy, wisdom, ideas."

Inspired by Bartholomew's cleverness, Barnabas, as if on
the campaign trail, forgot his painful past, looked at the audience, and like an all-knowing politician, said:

"Yes, most noble friends of this portentous courthouse!
Faced with the tears that fall during this all-too-brief show
called life, it behooves us to intoxicate ourselves with the wis-
dom of Jesus Christ, Confucius, Augustine, Rousseau, Auguste
Comte." And, looking in my direction as if to needle me, added,
"And of the great emperor Julius Caesar."

The audience of learned men applauded them vigorously.
I pulled Professor Jurema aside and muttered, "Professor, I
doubt they've ever read a book. They're just trying to win over
the crowd."

Jurema nodded, "The world belongs to the shrewd. They
grew up alone."

Barnabas had the audacity to tell the lawyers, "Esteemed
Mayor and distinguished attorneys, we mustn't forget Montesquieu and his great book *The Spirit of the Laws*."

Several of them knew who Montesquieu was. When they
heard that reference, they applauded the two shabby men more
enthusiastically. I felt the dreamseller should have been jealous of
those scene-stealers; after all, he carries the piano, tunes the piano,

plays the piano, and it's these buffoons who get the applause. But my cheeks burned when I saw the dreamseller was also clapping.

I was always an austere, stubborn professor who rarely laughed, very different from the dreamseller. He gives his disciples the freedom to do silly things, while I was a believer in absolute silence in the classroom. Respect above all. He wanted to disappear and allow the anonymous to stand out; I, on the other hand, never let any student win a debate. Obedience above all. I overvalued drama and disdained comedy in the small world of the classroom. The dreamseller valued both. I fear I prepared servants of the system rather than human beings to correct it. The dreamseller did the opposite.

That's when I noticed three men whispering next to me. They didn't realize I was part of the group. They were talking about the dreamseller. One of them took out a handheld computer and reviewed a series of images. I thought I saw the dreamseller on the screen. I tried to get closer, but they quickly removed the image. However, I was able to see a very strange message on the screen:

"The eagle lives. It must be destroyed." And they quietly left.

I remembered the dreamseller's revelations in the city's stadium: that he had been a giant in the financial and social world. But since he lived in tatters and was highly critical of the system in which we found ourselves, I took his revelations as symbolic, not literal. After watching him shiver from the lack of warm clothing, or get sick and not have medicine to treat his illness, or go hungry, I was convinced it was impossible he was once a multimillionaire. I figured he was a poor man who was rich in wisdom—but one who had no place to lay his head.

Then some teenagers in the audience bumped into me, trying to get closer to the dreamseller. They were students from a nearby school who had been passing by and were captivated by our two clowns.

Bartholomew and Barnabas, encouraged by the applause, took a bow. Then, Barnabas went into a trance, his politician's spirit once again taking over. He liked to use difficult words but often mispronounced them. As if in full campaign mode, he declared, "Hear me, people, the hoi polloi, the great unwashed masses of this noble city . . ."

"Yea! Very good!" bellowed Bartholomew, urging the crowd to break out in another round of applause. Extremely encouraged, the Mayor thanked them and continued his speech:

"I ask for your votes! I promise to clean up political skull-dugging." Barnabas gave a wan smile, unable to pronounce "skullduggery." He tried again and still got it wrong: "Skull-duggeny! Skulldugness!" And the more he spoke, the more he spat on those nearby. A judge came to his aid.

"Political *skullduggery*."

"Thank you, my future attorney-general," Barnabas said.

Edson, "the Miracle Worker," wasted no time. He took a cap from his jacket and brazenly added, "Well, good people, man does not live by talk alone. The Mayor, with that delicate little body of his, needs to eat. Who would like to contribute?" And he passed the cap among the onlookers, collecting enough money for a bountiful supper for the group.

The dreamseller left quietly. He was an artisan of ideas, while his two subordinates were artisans of eccentricity. But the lawyers remained thirsty for his knowledge. Some were already familiar with his reputation; now they knew his reasoning. They couldn't define him. Neither could we.

They understood, at least for the moment, that some write the laws, while others apply them. Some wear coats and ties, while others go around dressed in rags. Some write books, others read them. But fundamentally we are all children at play, not comprehending the most important phenomena of existence.

CHAPTER 5

A Master Who Disturbed the Brain

AS THE MONTHS PASSED, THE DREAMSELLER DEFENDED THE idea that the scientific discoveries that should free us were instead imprisoning us. Our minds were paralyzed by technology and excess information. We were like children living in the shadow of the "fathers of knowledge."

Pythagoras faced prejudice. Socrates submitted to the wrath of the Athenian elite. The world, symbolized by an apple, fell on Newton's head. Einstein had to disarm the bomb of truth while working in a patent office. Freud had to break the chains of a medicine that exalted the body at the expense of the mind.

The dreamseller argued that thinkers journeyed through pitfalls of injustice, disorder and lack of control on the road to true knowledge. We have forgotten this in our universities. We applauded courageous pioneers of knowledge but we were timid. We had a primal fear of confronting chaos and thinking freely.

"Don't blindly follow me. Don't swallow my ideas without letting them pass through the stomach of your criticism. Every great social and political disaster comes from the unquestioning worship of truth, the passive acceptance of ideas." Then what the dreamseller said shocked us: "The passive acceptance of ideas is worse than minor criticism aimed at them. I'm not looking for servants but followers who think. If they're not able to criticize me, they're not worthy of following me," he said emphatically.

Indignant, he said that the majority of students spent their twenty years from kindergarten to graduate school without ever formulating an original thought, without having opinions of their own and without the courage to think differently from their peers. We criticized the German youth who were seduced by Hitler to commit atrocities against Jews, Gypsies and homosexuals but were unaware that the social system was silencing the world's young people in our own century.

So one day, the dreamseller came onto the campus of one of the city's largest universities and shouted to the students:

"Venice is dying at the rate of half an inch a year. Doesn't that bother you? But who cares that the most charming of all cities is being drowned in the waters of the Adriatic? Where are the student protests against climatic disasters? Hunger kills between two hundred and three hundred poor, starving children daily. But who has time to listen to their cries? A small fraction of the funds world leaders spend to shore up the financial system could have wiped out world hunger. Doesn't such apathy bother you?"

Incensed, he would go from campus to campus, roaring:

"Fortunate are those who feed their brain with doubt, for theirs is the kingdom of new knowledge. Happy are those dissatisfied with our pitiful answers and false beliefs, for they arrive at places never before reached. Oh, how perverse a system that stones those who dare to think differently! Who will find solutions for the great problems of humanity?"

Some of the university students said, "What's that lunatic saying? Feeding the brain with doubt? We live in the time of scientific certainty and logic. How can anyone praise disorder?"

Seeing that none of the students raised their hands, Bartholomew stood up and said, "I'll try to solve the problems of humanity! I've been beaten down by society. I never fit into the normal way of doing things. I'm a wasted talent."

I couldn't believe his audacity. At the same time, the Mayor saw an eight-year-old boy drop his sandwich. The boy was the son of a professor standing a few yards away, concentrating on the bizarre characters who had invaded their campus.

The Mayor grabbed the sandwich, spat on it to clean it, rubbed it on his dirty clothes and then, with a subtle glance, offered it back to the little boy. The boy was disgusted and refused the sandwich. The Mayor began eating it like a starving dog. Between bites, he heard Honeymouth holding court and spoke up with his mouth full:

"Men like me, who personally know human suffering, should run the country." Lifting the remains of the sandwich he was eating, he added, "Don't be fooled by appearances. I'm an excellent product in a bad wrapper. Of the people and for the people, I sanctify myself."

I could keep quiet no longer. "'Sacrifice myself,'" I corrected him, "not 'sanctify myself.'"

Then the shameless reprobate looked at me and either praised or knocked me, I don't know which. "Saintly man! Thank you for your early vote. This man can see the pearl hidden in this handsome skull."

I raised my hands to my head and snorted to keep from lunging at him.

Days later, we were strolling casually down a wide street when we saw men and women in white clothing coming from and going into the convention center. A sign read "International Convention of Cardiology."

Without hesitating, the Master entered the lobby. We couldn't get into the private areas of the event because we didn't have badges, and given the clothes we were wearing any attempt to do so would lead to expulsion. I felt the setting was too sophisticated for us and tried to distance myself from the group.

The pharmaceutical industry, with luxurious booths, was displaying its latest heart medicines and inventions: antihypertensives, anticoagulants, antiarrhythmics and a whole series of other drugs and devices. Cardiology professors from countless medical schools from around the world were here. The dreamseller, with his trained eye, carefully observed their movement, their gestures, the muscles in their faces, their way of speaking. He noticed something strange.

A few minutes later, he decided to make his presence felt, raising his voice, regardless of whether he was making a scene or not.

"Distinguished cardiologists, you treat heart attacks and other coronary diseases. But who among you is healthy in his mental heart?"

Seeing that intriguing man with his booming voice and his crazy clothes talking to thin air, a small group of the curious soon gathered. Some thought he must be an actor hired to announce the launching of some new drug. But then came a bombshell:

"How many of you have mental arrhythmia or maybe even mental infarction? How many of you have an agitated mind, overactive, racing like a runaway heart? How many have emotions whose 'arteries' are as blocked as the coronaries that kill the tissues of the heart? Who among you relaxes and oxygenates his mind with pleasure?"

The audience of cardiologists had never heard such questions. Could the mind alter their intellectual pulse rate by generating an unhealthy overload of thoughts and mental images? The dreamseller believed it could. Could emotion block the flow of pleasure? He believed it could.

CHAPTER 6

Scream Therapy

THE DREAMSELLER'S KNOWLEDGE IMPRESSED ME. I DIDN'T know if he had an undergraduate degree or had done postgraduate studies, but I knew he read newspapers, magazines, scientific journals and books wherever he had a chance—even under bridges and overpasses, by candlelight. In fact, he kept small private libraries under two of the overpasses where we slept. A piece of bread satisfied him, but nothing nourished him like a good book. No one at the cardiology conference answered the dreamseller's questions. Though they remained silent, he knew that in many of the listeners' minds was a cry, an unheard cry indicating that something was amiss in their mental heart. They were overly agitated, excessively busy, thought too much and worked too hard. Like the businessmen, ninety percent of them had three or more psychosomatic symptoms such as headaches, accelerated heart rates, gastritis, hair loss attributable to stress, fatigue and memory loss.

"Can a person with mental heart disease take good care of someone with physical heart disease?" he asked. "Yes, he can. But not for long and not well."

Suddenly, a man appeared amid the small audience, bellowing so much that he almost gave them heart attacks. Yes, it was

Honeymouth, disturber of minds and hearts. He began screaming as if he were dying.

"Aaaahhh! Uuhhh! Aaaahhh! Uuhhh!" And then he fainted.

I went over to him, not knowing what was happening. For
a moment I thought, "This time Bartholomew's had a heart attack. Incredible, right in front of a group of cardiologists!" Solomon began to rub his hand on the left side of Bartholomew's
chest. I had to hold him up so he wouldn't pass out. Edson,
the Miracle Worker, kneeled and started praying for his dying
friend. Dimas panicked and said, "Honeymouth is going to die!
Honeymouth is going to die!" Monica and Jurema were in despair. They begged the doctors, "Help him, please! Don't let
him die!"

Bartholomew was immediately tended to by several doctors. They laid him on the floor and listened to his heart. A
doctor quickly brought a defibrillator to administer a shock.
The dreamseller was worried.

Suddenly, the Mayor rushed in. With total self-confidence,
as if he were the most experienced doctor on the planet, he said:

"Stay calm, my dear doctors. I'm familiar with the case.
He's my patient." Hearing this, they made way for him. He
abruptly grabbed Jurema by the hand and said, "This lovely
lady of some eighty-plus years will perform mouth-to-mouth
resuscitation on my patient."

"Me?" said the professor, startled.

Realizing that he was about to be kissed by Jurema, Bartholomew immediately sat up. Now, if it had been Monica, he
would have remained as still as a stone. Bartholomew opened
and closed his arms three times, breathing deeply, and gave
three small cries: "Aaahhh! Aaahhh!" Then he explained:

"My dear doctors, I have just done primal scream therapy.
A therapy that my friend Dr. Mayor and I created to de-stress
the heart!"

When they saw they'd been fooled, some of the cardiologists raised their hands to their heads. They felt like idiots, and so did I. Some of them reprimanded the pair; others wanted to punch them. The dreamseller had to intervene once again.

"Friends, have you noticed how our emotions can go from one extreme to the other in a fraction of a second? We're calm one instant, explosive the next. Peaceful one moment, aggressive the next. Isn't that a sign of mental collapse? Have you ever noticed how our mind suffers over foolish details, fluctuates because of small frustrations, taking on problems that aren't its own? Isn't that mental arrhythmia? Why get mad at these two young men? At least they tried to lower the stress level. They didn't hurt anyone."

In the field of sociology, we joked about surgeons, especially heart surgeons. Some of them had enormous egos. When they went into the operating room they thought they were gods, and when they left they were sure of it. Deep down, however, as the dreamseller tried to demonstrate, they were people who treated others with affection but were unaffectionate with themselves.

The doctors were speechless. They had never imagined that a beggar would tell them they had seriously fluctuating mental arrhythmia. And the dreamseller added, "The health care system has led you to partly betray the ethics of Hippocrates, the father of medicine: you took care of your patients but ignored yourselves . . ."

In fact, many doctors worked seventy-hour weeks. The excess of work conspired against their enjoyment of life. An elderly and experienced French professor of cardiology, already aware of the dreamseller's fame, took the liberty of speaking up:

"The incidence of cancer, heart disease, anxiety, panic attacks and depression among doctors is startling. We don't even have time to cry or lament."

A dismayed Brazilian heart surgeon added:

"It's true, the health care system has turned into a vampire that sucks the blood out of the most idealistic of professions. We spend our lives taking care of others and, before we know it, there's little time left for us to live. And the worst part is that we have to use our crumbs of time to reclaim the health we've lost along the way."

"If doctors themselves are sick," I thought, "then how bad off is the rest of the world?" I did a rundown of my past and remembered rarely meeting healthy, calm, sedate students and professors. And even the calm professors I knew had their fits of fury when contradicted. I, particularly, was tense, impatient, nervous, frenetic, angry. My emotions would go to extremes, from calm to irritable in a matter of seconds. I needed prescription tranquilizers to keep from erupting in the classroom, and just to sleep four or five hours a night—if I could sleep at all.

Just when the conversation was heading toward a higher plane, the Mayor asked a question to which I knew the answer: "Dreamseller, what do you think? Am I normal?"

This time, I laughed so hard that it startled the others. I couldn't hold back and told the dreamseller, "You're exceedingly normal, Mayor," if it was normal to be sick, I thought.

A smile plastered on his face, the Mayor said gratefully:

"Thank you, Julio Cesar, emperor of weary hearts. Someday, when I come to power, you will be my adviser for 'irrelevant' affairs."

I didn't know if I should be flattered or offended. All I know is that he managed to confuse me. While these thoughts were running through my mind, Bartholomew said to the Mayor:

"Wake up, Mayor! 'Superego' here called you a nutjob, batty, off your rocker. Get it?" Bartholomew had given me a nickname I hated: Superego. To that insulting alcoholic, "superego" meant superproud, superhaughty—not the way Freud conceived of it.

"Lay off, Honeymouth," the Mayor said. "You're the one who's unhinged." Infuriated, Honeymouth told the dream-seller, "You know I was a karate champion. Hold me back or that guy's going to get what's coming to him."

"Bring it on, you wimp."

Some of the doctors tried to separate these idiots. The Mayor took a boxer's stance, accidentally hitting the elderly French professor. Already stressed, fatigued and having gone several nights without sleep, the doctor fainted.

"Oh, no! I've sent the doctor to meet his maker," he said.

I raised my hands to my head, feeling partially responsible. Society was already smothering doctors, and we were making it worse. The world was one gigantic mental hospital, and the dreamseller's disciples were setting fire to it. The doctor quickly regained consciousness, stood up and began screaming:

"Aaaahhh! Uuhhh! Aaaahhh! Uuhhh!"

Everyone tried to help him, but suddenly, after the primi-tive grunts, he spread his arms, breathed deeply and said, "Take it easy, people. It's scream therapy! It *does* feel great to de-stress!"

Two other doctors also began screaming. Immediately, other formal, extremely well-behaved physicians started to shout. Security called the paramedics.

For a crazy moment, I had the urge to let out some screams of my own to relieve my stress. Craziness, I discovered, is con-tagious.

CHAPTER 7

A Psychotic with Quite an Imagination

W E SLEPT THAT NIGHT BENEATH THE AMERICA BRIDGE, which connected to the city's major arteries. It wasn't the place where we usually slept, since the nightly traffic of buses and trucks was nearly unbearable. But we had a reserved spot in that enormous "hotel" for the homeless, where we kept a few thin mattresses in a corner. No one touched our meager belongings, for among the homeless there's a code of mutual protection: each one respects the crumbs of the other.

Geronimo, an elderly and likable beggar who had been sleeping at the America for twenty years, liked it when we spent the night there. He would perk up when we arrived, serving us stale crackers and cookies. Incredible as it seems, he made delicious coffee over a small campfire. He was schizophrenic and, from time to time, he hallucinated. During those attacks, he would talk about the monsters that pursued him. His imagination would be the envy of horror story writers. While we drank coffee, he told us that the night before he had faced the most terrifying monster:

"The beast had seven heads with seven horns. He had a sword in his hands and another that stuck out of his belly. I could see his heart beating in his chest. And he sucked the blood out of anything that came near him. The monster howled like a dinosaur. He wanted to eat me alive. He was as hungry as the Mayor and as ugly as the Miracle Worker," he said, pointing at Edson. We nearly died laughing.

Geronimo's mind was sometimes a scattered mess. He interrupted the story of the monster and started telling us about an airplane that had flown under the bridge. Bartholomew said anxiously, "Wait, what did you do about the beast?"

Like Don Quixote recalling windmills, Geronimo remembered the story. He puffed out his chest and finished his epic tale:

"I fought the demon for two hours. That beast with his two large swords and me with just this little knife." He showed us the blade as if it were his trophy. "The monster was angry. He jumped around like a monkey and talked like Honeymouth: 'I'll kill you, old man! This overpass belongs to me!' It was a battle of giants. He almost cut open my chest, almost gashed my neck, almost fractured my skull. Almost, but I was more agile than the beast. As quick as a cat, I stabbed him in the back. And seeing that he couldn't defeat me, the monster ran away."

Bartholomew said enthusiastically, "Next time you come and get me, Geronimo, and I'll get rid of it. I used to be a monster hunter under these bridges."

"Right," I thought to myself, "you hunted the monsters you created when you were having alcohol withdrawal symptoms." I had witnessed one of those attacks.

"You can count on me, too," said the Mayor. "I've killed ten tyrannosaurs in my time."

The Mayor went on to demonstrate to Geronimo just how he had dispatched those fierce animals. Awkward as always, he tripped and landed on top of the poor old man, knocking him off his feet. We helped Barnabas up and he pulled Geronimo from the rubble. Regaining his composure, the old man said:

"Rest assured I'll call you the next time the monster shows up . . ." He paused, then concluded, "Actually, maybe I'll just wait and watch that fight on television."

I chuckled. Even Geronimo wanted to get away from the pair. I don't know whether they believed his story, whether they had psychotic attacks of their own, or if they were just up for anything that promised a bit of amusement. All I do know is that one lunatic understands another.

The next morning, I got up early with an aching back. My monster was the mattress pad. We said good-bye to Geronimo and resumed our journey. Three blocks later, we saw an apparently nervous man coming toward us. He was about forty and had slightly graying hair, a light complexion and was wearing a white shirt and black blazer. He could have been another of the dreamseller's admirers—or one of his critics.

The dreamseller, the Mayor, Bartholomew and I were just ahead of the group, and Professor Jurema and Monica had just caught up with us. We were telling them about Geronimo's feats and when the stranger came up to him and said:

"Dreamseller, I've got a present for you." He immediately put his hand inside his blazer and pulled out a revolver. Just as he was about to fire point-blank, the dreamseller, with impressive reflexes, knocked the gun from his hand, tossed it into the air and caught it. We were amazed. The astonished criminal ran off.

"Please bury this," the dreamseller told Bartholomew, handing him the gun.

"How did you do that?" Edson asked.

Smiling, he replied, "Experience. I'm an expert in certain kinds of hand-to-hand combat."

"Are you joking?" Solomon asked in surprise.

"Life is one big joke," he said, and went on walking.

Meanwhile, the Mayor was busy hurting another innocent

bystander. As he told the story of the dreamseller grabbing the gun, he thrust his right fist forward and brought his left elbow back quickly, yelling "Yah!" and unwittingly hit Jurema in the stomach. She fell backward.

"Oh, God, I've killed Jurema!"

But Jurema didn't die. She had practiced ballet for more than thirty years and had sharp reflexes. When she saw the Mayor's elbow, she managed to pull back and cushion the blow. We rushed to her side.

"The Mayor's going to kill one of us yet," she said, as we helped her up.

I started to think about the danger the dreamseller had exposed himself to. I was especially worried about the way the guy had approached him. He didn't look like a mugger, more like an assassin. It looked like a hit job. But who would want to kill him, and why? I had little time to think about the matter, however, because the dreamseller soon offered us some more beautiful lessons.

He saw an olive tree that was over three hundred years old. Its gnarled trunk was twisted and mutilated by the effects of weather over the centuries. Contemplating it joyfully, he said:

"Olive tree, you are stronger than the strongest of men. How many generals have passed by you, proud, arrogant, as if they were immortal, but succumbed to the perils of time? And you, humbly, have endured. How many kings have passed by you with majestic processions, only to face certain ruin? And you, simple and nameless, endure to this day, continuing to tell your story."

He turned to us and said, "The best stories are written in anonymity. It's time for the anonymous revolution."

Along our journey, I suspected that the dreamseller wished to bring about a revolution in the fabric of society. A revolution of ideas, one without weapons. A simple, implosive, penetrating revolution, but one without pressure, coercion, manipulation or aggression. However, considering the team he had chosen to carry out that revolution, I felt he had already failed. Could it be he didn't realize that the complicated group of disciples wasn't up to the task? Who would listen to them? Do politicians listen to a band of troublemakers? Would Congress treat them like clowns or wise men?

But I didn't realize that the sparks of revolution had already been lit. Not only were his disciples more outspoken in debating ideas, countless people who would follow us were braver, no longer lowering their heads when confronted, exercising their rights, feeling like citizens.

The ideas he offered went viral. I was not the only one writing them down, so were journalists and students. They were beginning to think critically, to construct ideas of their own and to have the audacity to express them.

CHAPTER 8

The Great Mission

TWO WEEKS LATER, WE WENT BACK TO THE ENORMOUS courtyard outside the federal courthouse. This time the dreamseller did not address an audience. He sat down on the grass in silence, near an old concrete bench with peeling paint. He gazed calmly at the horizon as if both close to and distant from us. We sat down around him and I was glad to not have a crowd around us.

The dreamseller brushed his hair away from his brow and said softly:

"Rousseau said that man is born good and society corrupts him. But that idea needs some refining: to me, *man is born neutral and society educates or accentuates his instincts, frees his mind or imprisons it. And it usually imprisons it.*"

The dreamseller was always warning us that we must seek the true breath of freedom. We were suffocated by the shrinking of pleasure, creativity and spontaneity.

"Every baby," he continued, "is born with an instinct for aggressiveness and selfishness. It's a parent's job to polish that mind by filling it with thousands of life experiences to mitigate those primal instincts and breed altruism, compassion, friendliness and the ability to think before acting."

Hearing his words, I sifted through my own memory. I had

met many social scientists and authors but never anyone like
this. I wondered if I was seeing history in the making. I asked
myself how far this revolutionary dreamseller would go with
his plan and whether the texts I'd write about him would reach
the people.

At that moment, Edson, the Miracle Worker, suddenly ran
up, panting, almost out of breath. He had gone to use the bath-
room, and as he walked back, he happened upon a scene that
shook him. Nervously, he told us about a young man climbing
the thirty-foot high monument to independence, most likely to
take his own life. People were gathering anxiously around the
site.

A chill ran down my spine. I remembered when I was at
the top of the San Pablo Building, depressed, hopeless, with no
reason to go on living. Images flashed through my mind, images
I wanted to erase but couldn't. The past can't be erased. It only
assumes other guises.

The news shook our group. We all looked at the dreamseller. We expected he would immediately rise to his feet and
rescue the young man, as he had done with me. But he didn't
move. We expected he would use his incisive intelligence to
break through the resistance of a youth who had lost the en-
chantment of life. But he didn't react. We tried to lead him by
the arm, but he insisted on staying where he was.

To our amazement, he told us, "Go there and sell dreams to
the man."

"What? Us? It's too big a risk, Master!" Monica said, and
we all agreed.

The simple thought of someone killing themselves right before our eyes, and our being unable to do anything about it
unnerved us. We were imprisoned by fear.

Tears are shed at the beginning and the end of life, but it's
hard to witness a young person cutting off his own breath. Who

is he? Who are his friends? What torments him? We were unprepared to confront that volatile situation. What if we failed?

The dreamseller remained seated. Seeing us rooted alongside him, he recited the poetry of dreams:

"Dreams inspire emotion, free the imagination, nurture the
intelligence. Whoever dreams rewrites his story and reinvents
his history. Will you reinvent yourselves?"

Suddenly, his emotions flashed, he stood up and finished
his thought:

"Without dreams, we're the servants of selfishness, vassals
of individualism, slaves to our instincts. The greatest dream to
be sold in this society is the dream of a free mind!"

"Do you dream of a free mind?" he yelled, startling passersby. "If you dream, why don't you take risks to rescue that
young man? The risk of failing, of looking ridiculous, of being
embarrassed, of crying, being labeled stupid, psychotic, a fraud
are all part of being a dreamseller. And that's why I have called
you!"

And he urged us:

"That man doesn't want to kill himself. He has a thirst to
live but doesn't know it. Use his self-destructive energy to
explore his thirst. How? I don't know! Free his mind! Do the
dance of life. Approach him with a flexible, loose, imaginative
mind."

I tried to gulp down the knot in my throat. This is one thing
a university never taught me to do.

"Dancing's something I understand!" Honeymouth said.
And that's just what I was afraid of.

"And so do I!" said the Mayor, suddenly grabbing Monica
to dance.

A man was dying, and these two found time to play.

CHAPTER 9

Good Samaritans or Funeral Home Partners?

———

W E WEREN'T PRIESTS OR DOCTORS, AND CERTAINLY NOT psychologists. We weren't perfect or self-confident, and we had no experience in rescuing depressed people. We were just people, fascinated by a stranger who used every means to free us from the place where we were imprisoned.

The dreamseller's words played in my mind. I couldn't remain indifferent, especially since I had come close to killing myself under similar circumstances. But I was paralyzed. "But why am I paralyzed?" I wondered. "From fear that the man will kill himself or from fear that I won't be able to help him?"

It bothered me to realize that my fear of failure mattered more to me than this man's life. I had spent years speaking about freedom while being imprisoned by this society. I was a critical intellectual and, as such, thought that critics were free, but critics rarely stick their necks out. They hide their shortcomings. I needed to try, needed to go beyond the frontiers of my ego, but my legs wouldn't obey. Stress shook the balance between my brain and my body.

What now, I thought: Do I react or retreat? Hold out my hands or pull them back? Face the shame or hide? I needed to make a choice and accept the consequences. I had made a thousand excuses for not reaching out to help others in the past. But now I was out of excuses.

Solomon was hyperventilating at the thought, rubbing his hands on his chest. He asked the Mayor to sit down, and thankfully, he came to his senses. Noting our hesitancy, the dreamseller asked once more, "Who will go?"

Professor Jurema rubbed her forehead. I lowered my eyes. Edson mediated. Dimas snorted. "Send me, Boss. I accept the challenge," Bartholomew said.

Barnabas rose and said, "Dreamseller, count me in. I'm a freethinker, so how can I refuse to free other minds?"

I thought I was going to have a panic attack. A closeted atheist, I found myself calling on the divine. "Oh my God, not those two!"

But the pair was emboldened. Resolute, they rose to their feet. And foreseeing the worst, I tried to warn the dreamseller as politely as I could.

"Bartholomew and Barnabas are good, well-meaning guys who like to help their fellow man. But don't you think it's better for them to stay here?"

They wrinkled their noses.

"Why are you worried, Superego?" they responded unflinchingly.

I couldn't take it. I forgot about the guy on the verge of killing himself:

"Why am I worried? For a million of reasons," I replied, irritated. "You can't control your tongue! You're impertinent, insubordinate, rebellious. With the two of you, what's already a difficult task will become mission impossible!"

"I know that movie!" the Mayor yelled.

Although Jurema had been more patient than I, she couldn't stand it anymore, either. She feared these two recovering alcoholics would ruin the dreamseller's plan: The revolution of the anonymous would never strike a blow.

"Master, I really like Bartholomew and Barnabas, but you're the only one with enough experience to keep this man from committing suicide."

But all of this only made the two more determined.

"My dear and lovely Jurema, esteemed Superego, please remain calm. Barnabas and I are experts at dealing with suicides."

"We are?" Barnabas asked. But then he coughed and corrected himself: "I mean, yes, of course we are. We've already sent ten to their graves."

"Ten?" I asked, thinking it must be a joke.

"Yes, ten!" confirmed the inveterate talker, spreading his hands.

We almost fainted when we heard this statistic, but no one doubted they had sent ten people to meet their maker. Just imagine if they had tried to save me when I wanted to give up on life. I'd be gone. I ran a hand over my head and neck to reassure myself I was alive. The lump was still in my throat.

Monica, ever patient and amused, had a soft spot for the two of them, but she knew they had no place in a situation that called for calm, clear thinking.

"Dreamseller, I hoped that with time your disciples would become calmer, restrained, balanced. But some of them seem . . . not quite ready."

I don't know whether Bartholomew understood her criticism, but he was grateful. "Thank you, dear Monica."

The Master replied patiently:

"Monica, no one can change anyone else. My plan isn't to change them but to encourage them to rewrite their story. Wisdom doesn't lie in changing others but in respecting our differences."

Edson, the Miracle Worker, was anxious, thinking about the young man who had scaled the monument. After a few silent prayers, he tried flattery:

"Honeymouth, Mayor, you're the most gifted of the group. I suggest you stay with the dreamseller while we try to do something for this poor man . . ."

Even Dimas, aka Angel Hand, a skilled pickpocket and recovering rogue, tried to stop them. Dimas, who was stuttering less and less, began stammering again. "I'll st-stay wi—with you, dear fr—friends."

But nothing deterred the determined duo. The Mayor, sticking out his chest like a politician, proclaimed, "Voices of the opposition wish to silence me!"

"You're only hearing the voices in your head," I said, unable to restrain myself.

"Trust in God and in us, too," Honeymouth said.

The dreamseller shook his head. We were wasting time squabbling. "Arguments are excuses for inaction! Let them go. You're a family.

"Be social activists. Act."

For the first time, I realized how demagogues are created; we had fallen victim to something I had dedicated so much time railing against in my writings. It was time to act.

Bartholomew tried to put us at ease. "Rest assured, my friends. Ours are complex minds in search of the uncomplicated. We'll only come to the rescue if the rest of you fail."

"How can we stop them?" I asked Monica and Jurema. "Those two are nothing but trouble."

And they would cause much more trouble than we ever imagined.

CHAPTER 10

Paralyzed by Fear

LIVING IN OUR DYSFUNCTIONAL FAMILY MEANT CONSTANT surprises, sometimes spectacular, sometimes pathetic. Young Solomon and Edson took me by the arm and hurried me along. We wondered whether we might be too late.

On the way to the other end of the square, we passed dozens of towering trees—pine trees, palms, and acacias—blocking our view of the cast-iron horse the man had scaled. On the way, Bartholomew decided, "Superego, you'll be our leader!"

"Leader? Me? Fat chance!" I said. But they all wanted me to lead the mission. After all, I was the one with the most personal experience with this. But my mind was racing, my fragile courage stripped from me, my spirits stolen away. I thought, "What can I say? And how to say it? How should I act? This was going to be a catastrophe."

Barnabas was so overweight and out of shape he was out of breath and lagged behind. "It takes one to save one," he said between bites of a sandwich.

I wanted to pummel him, but I tried to regain control. For years on end I prepared tirelessly for every class I taught, but now I was in uncharted water. And I wished I had a compass. Just then, Bartholomew looked at the group and said, "People. Let's pretend we're normal."

Monica replied tensely, "Then hide your face and shut your mouth, Bartholomew."

Despite how nervous they made me, Don Quixote and Sancho Panza—Honeymouth and his faithful squire, the Mayor—were invariably festive. "There are advantages to being that crazy," I told myself.

As we neared the monument, we saw people clustered around the base. I looked up and saw a man younger than thirty years old near the top. Knowing the dreamseller was nowhere near to help me, my anxiety clouded my thoughts.

Monica and Jurema trailed behind me, breathlessly, followed by Bartholomew and Barnabas, who were chatting about trivial matters.

Honeymouth asked for a bite of the Mayor's sandwich. And the Mayor, realizing it was almost gone, guarded it like a lion with its prey. I couldn't understand how they could eat at a time like this. More than a hundred people had formed a semi-circle in front of the monument. The fireman hadn't arrived yet. A few policemen were patrolling the courtyard of the federal courthouse, but they had no idea what to do. The jumper had already made his way up the sixty-foot pedestal and was now climbing up the gigantic cast-iron horse. All he had was a grapple and a rope for support. He slipped frequently, making the onlookers gasp. He didn't appear to be an amateur rock climber or thrill-seeker, just a human being in the terminal stages of pain.

Bartholomew and Barnabas looked at me and said, "Well, leader, what now?"

I didn't know where to begin. I saw myself in him, sensed myself in him but was at a loss for what to do or how to get him to come down. It only managed to awaken the demons slumbering in my unconscious. They no longer haunted me, but it was uncomfortable to revive them.

I knew the young man wanted to find a place that existed only in his limited imagination, a place without pain, tears, memories—nothing. He must have tried to overcome his problems and perhaps had taken medication or alcohol in search of relief. He must have heard advice and sought alternatives to ease his troubled mind. But nothing had comforted him, apparently. Language is a crude instrument when it comes to describing a crisis. When I passed through the arduous valley of clinical depression, I was a stranger even to myself.

Monica grabbed my arm. She had once been a slave to bulimia; she would binge eat and then purge. Her self-image was distorted. As a model, she was applauded for her beauty, but her self-esteem was nonexistent. On this day, she urged me to take action:

"Quick, you have to do something. He's going to jump at any moment."

I didn't want the burden of being the leader. After all, I wasn't even the leader of myself. I'm a genius, and like many geniuses, I have faith only in science and in numbers, not in life. Though I have an IQ of 140, far above average, that IQ hadn't humanized me. I still couldn't manage to take a risk for the young man. What good is a high IQ if I can't think straight when the world is crumbling around me? What good does it do to have an extraordinary cerebral cortex if I react like a child in tense situations?

When I turned and found Edson praying, I snapped at him. "Stop praying," I said, "and show us your miraculous powers!"

Since I wasn't taking any action, others more human than I risked themselves. Bartholomew was actually behaving himself, realizing there was very little he could do. Trying to unblock my mind, he asked, "How did the dreamseller rescue you?"

I remembered how he had broken through the police tape

and gone to the top of the building, sneaking past the psychiatrist and the police chief. When he approached me, I screamed
that I would kill myself. But he unnerved me when he sat down
on the ledge and began eating a sandwich. I shouted again that
I would end my life, but he astonished me by saying, "Could
you not interrupt my dinner?" I remember thinking, "I've met
somebody crazier than I am."

When I told Bartholomew that the Dreamseller had begun
his rescue with nothing but a sandwich in his hand, the Mayor
jumped in. He took his sandwich from his old black coat and
presented it to me, saying "It's up to you, my friend!"

It was like a 10,000 volt shock. I swallowed hard. I didn't
know what to do with that sandwich or how to start my inter-
vention. I only knew that I could very well hasten this man's
suicide. I had lived that story and I knew banal words are useless.

I had to use something unexpected to break into his con-
flicted mind, as the dreamseller had done with me. But it didn't
come to me. My anxiety paralyzed my body and mind. I began
to exhibit nervous tics, blinking my eyes, and rubbing my face
compulsively. I was stripped of my pride in public.

CHAPTER 11

A Devilish Confusion

WHILE I FLOUNDERED, OTHERS TRIED TO DO WHAT I COULD not—save the young man. Professor Jurema, the most daring, shouted up at him, "Life is hard, son, but don't give up on it. Fight back!"

Nothing. The man didn't even react. Another woman, who appeared to be about seventy-five, called up to him: "Think about the people who love you."

But he remained unmoved. This was a man who was tired of thinking, of caring and he saw none of the beauty in life. His sole desire was to end his emotional suffering.

A psychologist stepped forward from the crowd, went up to the monument, and tried to draw his attention. "Please, give me the chance to listen to you! You have a friend in me. Let's talk!"

It was an interesting, respectful, intelligent approach. But the man didn't want friends or to talk about his problems. Resolute in his decision, he wasn't seeking opportunities to find relief. When he had almost reached the horse's back, he stumbled and nearly fell. Panicked people covered their eyes.

Two psychiatrists who specialized in prescribing antidepressants were passing by and stopped to try to help. They conferred with each other but didn't know how to proceed. They were successful in medicating cooperative patients but were at a loss in a situation like this.

One of the doctors, a gray-haired man, ventured the obvious: "Don't take your life. There's no suffering that can't be overcome."

But the young man seemed deaf, hearing only the voice in his nightmares. Others tried: a policeman, a cardiologist, a social worker. All failed. The young man looked down and finally spoke, shouting angrily at the spectators, "Get out of here if you don't want to see a man's final moments."

He had climbed atop the horse and was trying to reach the shoulders of the soldier. Suddenly, he lost his grip and started to fall off the side, clutching onto the soldier's sword with one hand. The crowd gasped. He continued scaling the monument, unaware that unconsciously he wanted to scale the heights of his anguish and transcend it. He wanted to jump from the highest point. I saw this as a breath of life, a spark of hope. And I tried to use it to save his life.

I pushed aside my fears and attempted to win him over by putting myself in his place. I took a deep breath and said, "Listen, my friend! I've been where you are. I understand, at least a little, the pain you must be going through. Tell me your stories, your troubles. Life is worth the trouble."

The young man stopped climbing. I thought I had reached him. But I was quickly disillusioned.

"Your words make me want to throw up."

I was shaken. I saw that I'd done worse than the others. Nothing seemed to move him. He finally made it to the top of the monument and stood on the shoulders of the iron soldier. It was hard for him to keep his balance.

That was when the two "gravediggers" of the group showed

up at the worst possible moment. Both came dangerously close to the monument and, instead of speaking to the jumper, started trying to calm the crowd.

"Take it easy, folks! Don't lose hope!" said Honeymouth.

"We're going to get this guy down in a hurry," the Mayor said.

The crowd fell silent. The young man was flabbergasted. He looked down, blinked, and couldn't believe what he heard. "Do those guys want to see blood?" he must have thought. I looked at him and immediately put my hands over my eyes.

Suddenly, Honeymouth began to shout like a lunatic. "Come down from there so I can kick your ass," he said.

Everyone, from the crowd to the young man, was shocked—speechless. There was no doubt these two were out of their minds.

"Right! Just because you climbed that monument you think you're hot stuff? Come on down from there so I can slap you around," the Mayor added, and started making karate moves.

The scene was so absurd that the suicide thought he must be delirious. He shook his head to see if he was hearing right.

Without missing a beat, Honeymouth yelled, "Suffering is a privilege of the living, you jerk. Face your life, you pile of Jell-O. Come down here and I'll smack you around a little to wake you up."

We almost fainted. I saw the color drain from the faces of the rest of the group. All of us were astonished. Once again I asked myself what I was doing in that group.

I was convinced those two were born to be partners in a funeral home. They weren't selling dreams; they were selling coffins. I imagined the guy jumping from the monument and landing at our feet. I felt the urge to pounce on Bartholomew and Barnabas and gag them.

The Mayor went even further. He began to scoff at the reasons that people kill themselves.

"What are you afraid of, huh? That you're in a financial hole? I'm in a deeper one. There's over a hundred bill collectors on my tail, son."

The man atop the monument writhed with rage. Then, seemingly indifferent to the young man, Honeymouth started chatting with the Mayor. The would-be suicide paid attention to their conversation, spoken loudly enough for him to understand what was being said.

"Mayor, every time I pass a bank, I make the sign of the cross and feel like sending flowers."

"Why, Honeymouth?"

"Because that's where I'm buried."

Both broke into laughter. Those nearby laughed at these clowns, momentarily forgetting they were at a horror show.

"I'd need to send an entire florist shop, man," the Mayor added.

Seeing them first humiliate each other and then collapse in laughter, the suicide trembled with anger. He didn't know whether to kill himself or them. They were stealing the scene. As if this weren't enough, Honeymouth began speaking of other reasons people kill themselves.

"Wake up, kid! What, did you make a fool of yourself? Did somebody insult you? Do wrong by you? I've been there. I've been kicked out, handcuffed, tied up, imprisoned. They say I'm a hopeless bum, an incorrigible nut, a characterless drunk."

"But you *are* all that, Honeymouth."

"Am I? Yeah, I guess you're right." Then he resumed his verbal assault on the young man. "You're running away from your little depression! I've been through one of the biggest. Even my shrink couldn't put up with me. Did your wife cheat on you? I've been cheated on five times!"

The young man's face was starting to twitch with rage. He scratched his head, snorted, wished he had wings so he could fly down and pummel these two.

"Five women cheated on you, Honeymouth?"

"Five, Mayor. The women don't know what they missed out on. *C'est la vie,* my friend," he said, mixing French and English.

Then it was the Mayor's turn to attack. "Are you running away from your mother-in-law? I've taken crap from three of them. One of them tried to shove my head into a microwave!"

The crowd again forgot the young man and laughed. Some began to believe it was all a show by some local theater group.

"But you *are* a scoundrel, Mayor. You deserve to be cooked alive," said Bartholomew, turning his back on the young man.

The Mayor claimed he was innocent, and to leave no room for doubt, related some of his run-ins with his former mothers-in-law. "I'd rather go to war than face a crazy mother-in-law."

Atop the monument, the young man's lips were twisted in rage. He looked like a lion trying to roar.

"You wanna die 'cause you've suffered losses? I've lost more than you have, you wimp! I lost father, mother, brother, wife, uncles, cousins, friends, jobs, respect, home."

"And even your sense of shame," the Mayor added.

"But I never lost faith in life!" Bartholomew said defiantly.

Then the Mayor began bouncing around like a boxer. He leaped and punched the air, saying, "Come on down here and face my fist of fury, you little worm!" And, like the lousy fighter he was, he tripped over his own feet, stuck out his right fist, and unintentionally hit Honeymouth on the chin.

"Where am I?" Honeymouth said, staggering. Dizzy, he blinked, saw Monica, and said, "What a lovely place. I must be in heaven." Then he looked at me, came to his senses, and said, "What's so funny, Superego? You never took one on the chin from a friend?" And he rubbed his jaw.

Solomon began to feel his obsessive-compulsive urge to stick his forefinger into a hole. But he couldn't find any available orifice. Suddenly, he noticed Edson, the Miracle Worker, praying for an angel to rescue the young man. He saw the available opening and stuck his finger deep inside it. Edson leaped forward and bellowed:

"Be gone from this body, evil spirit!" he said, thinking it was a demon trying to possess him.

I shouldn't have laughed at such a tense moment, but I couldn't hold back. I covered my mouth to avoid an explosive guffaw.

Fortunately, the police showed up to put an end to the festivities. They grabbed and handcuffed the two troublemakers and were about to haul them off to the precinct for attempted manslaughter. The young man was ecstatic as he watched; now he could finally kill himself in peace.

But suddenly Professor Jurema stepped forward.

She had white hair, a face marked by the passing of time but was dressed impeccably with beige pants and a crisp white blazer, and gave off the air of someone trustworthy. "Take it easy, officers, take it easy. These two are family."

The cops didn't understand, but they stopped to listen. She explained: "We're one big family."

"What? You, these two, and the guy up there on the monument are all related?" the confused policemen asked.

"Sure," she said, hugging Bartholomew and Barnabas. "Can't you see the resemblance?" Then, addressing the two nutty disciples, she said, "Don't you worry, boys. I'm here."

"You sure the jumper up there is one of you, too?" the taller of the two cops, a muscular dark-complexioned man, asked Honeymouth.

"My younger brother."

Hearing this, the jumper was so angry he thought he was going to have a heart attack.

And that's how the strangest family ever to walk the earth was formed.

CHAPTER 12

A Really Crazy Family

THE POLICEMEN FREED OUR FRIENDS. THEY MIGHT HAVE doubted the two men, but not the elderly woman. Barnabas led Bartholomew by the arm and together they whispered to Jurema, "He's part of the family?"

"Yes."

"But what family?" Bartholomew asked, curious.

"This family of lunatics, for heaven's sake!" Professor Jurema said.

"Hey, you're right!" He looked up and said, "I even feel like I know that guy."

The jumper was curious about what was going on beneath his feet. He tried to turn his ear to the wind to hear their whispers as the two troublemakers thanked Jurema:

"Thank you, Granny!"

Sure, Jurema was old enough to be their grandmother, but she didn't take well to being called that. "Granny? No, Mom's more like it."

Her words tapped something lost in them. Both had been abandoned by their parents. Upon being adopted in public by the professor, they started kissing her. Perhaps with an eye to an inheritance, they told her:

"Mommy, we love you. You saved us!" Jurema tried desperately to get them off her.

"All right, all right! Enough! I'm Granny, okay? Forget I said anything."

The scene was so bizarre that the young man was no longer the center of attention but just a supporting character. He was now part of the confused audience watching this ragtag team of dreamsellers.

Solomon, Dimas, Monica and Edson all began to hug and kiss Jurema and call her Granny. I was the only one who kept my distance.

At that moment, Barnabas once again caught the spirit. Turning to the crowd, he tried to explain the inexplicable. "Noble members of the public, fear not. We're simply resolving a family matter. The guy up there is our brother."

The jumper was dumbstruck. He was so angry he was almost spitting fire. Being insulted by these two vagrants was one thing, but being adopted into a family of nutjobs was too much to bear. He lost the will to die. All he wanted was to focus his anger on these loons and end their little circus. But he thought he had gone too far to give up. So he decided to watch the events unfold.

To make things worse, Jurema decided to climb on the shoulders of her two stooges. Their alcoholic pasts had left them with the worst sense of balance. She almost fell several times, but thanks to the ballet classes she took in her youth, she kept her balance.

I expected her to be gentle with the young man. Boy, was I wrong. "Get down from there, you miscreant! Come to Granny so I can spank that pale little butt of yours."

I couldn't believe what I was hearing. Professor Jurema, a woman with a doctorate in psychology, a noted writer highly respected in academic circles, had come down to Bartholomew and Barnabas's level? I nearly fainted.

When he heard the old lady challenging him, the man became dizzy, the world began to spin around him. He got so woozy that he fell and landed—hard—straddling the horse's hindquarters.

Solomon cringed. "P-poor guy, now he's st-sterile, too."

The expression on the young man's face was at first inscrutable . . . and then suddenly tortured. He looked down and emitted a war cry: "Aaaargh!"

"Hey, he's using our scream therapy, Honeymouth," the Mayor said.

The man didn't know whether to cry or scream or kill himself. I looked at him and realized that his brain was paralyzed by testicular pain. He was as motionless as the statue.

"Come on down, little brother," Honeymouth said. "If you don't, I'm gonna climb up and grab you by the arm." And, looking at Jurema, he said dramatically, "Hold me back, Granny, or I'm climbing this thing!"

"No, don't do that," she begged him.

"No! It's too dangerous!" Edson added.

The crowd shifted. The only thing worse than witnessing one death was watching two.

"Mayor, I'm gonna end this once and for all," Honeymouth declared.

The Mayor called his bluff. "An excellent idea. Godspeed!"

Honeymouth gulped. "Well, only because Granny insists, I'll stay. I'm staaaaying!" he yelled up to the young man.

He walked close to the Mayor and whispered, "You'll pay for this, you rat!"

While they were arguing, the young man rushed down the monument to settle his debts. He was panting, in a frenzy by the time he reached the ground. Jurema, frightened, ran to hide behind Monica and me.

Bartholomew and Barnabas hadn't realized the young man had come down and was rushing up to them. The crowd applauded when he reached the ground, but the two thought the applause was for their heroism. Their backs to the monument and facing the audience, they bowed their heads in acknowlcdgment.

Raising his right hand to the heavens and lifting his voice like a politician, Barnabas launched into a short speech:

"Thank you for the most distinguished homage, my generous people. I pledge to issue a decree destroying all the monuments in the city so that no future idiot can try to kill himself."

The Mayor didn't know that the young man was standing right next to him, ready to explode. We all closed our eyes. This, we couldn't watch. Just then, Honeymouth made things even worse.

"No, not idiot! Jackass!" And he turned to put his hands on the shoulder of the guy next to him—unaware that it was the young man.

Trembling with rage, the young man said, "Who *are* you?"

The bungling buffoon tried to imitate the dreamseller's deep quotations. "Who am I? I don't know. I'm simply in search of myself."

"Yeah? Well, now you've found me!"

But before the young man could make a move, the Mayor, looking up at the statue, was startled to see that the jumper wasn't there. "Honeymouth! Our brother's gone to meet his maker!" he yelled.

Little did they know he was inches away from punching their own one-way tickets.

CHAPTER 13

The Great Surprise

THE YOUNG MAN WAS MASSIVE IN STATURE. BLOND, HUSKY, muscular, with powerful arms and a chest chiseled from working out. He was a professional boxer—a heavyweight. He stood almost six feet tall and weighed two hundred and ten pounds. He grabbed Bartholomew and Barnabas each by the collars and told them:

"Get ready to meet your maker, you jackasses!" he said. And then the boxer started pummeling our friends.

No one had any idea what was going on. Most thought it was bad blood between brothers. We jumped on the young boxer and managed to prevent a massacre. Even the cops joined the melee. Once they were separated, Honeymouth, bleeding and confused, groggily asked his buddy, "Mayor, are we in heaven?"

"I suspect we're in hell," Barnabas replied.

When the two realized the brute was the man from the monument, they fell to the ground on their knees. It seemed like they were thanking God for still being alive.

Jurema whispered to Monica. I could read her lips saying "This was their plan, all along." "How ridiculous," I thought. There was no way these two idiots could have consciously used such a tactic to save the young man. *Or could they?*

I began to bombard myself with questions. "Aren't these two total imbeciles? Thoughtless loudmouths? These guys can't account for their own actions, much less some one else's. How could they have outsmarted everyone and used an actual strategy to rescue him?"

I turned to see them still on their knees, mouthing the word "eleventh." I was shocked. And the windows to my mind opened. It's not easy to break through the walls of prejudice, but I began to see their actions from a different angle. I finally understood how they reached him. They had provoked him to the point of rage so that he would focus on punishing them instead himself—something I would never have considered.

They didn't use philosophical words as the dreamseller did to rescue me from the top of the San Pablo Building, but they did use the same passion, the same surprise attack, the same ability for disarming the mind and demolishing false arguments. I was amazed.

Later we would learn that Bartholomew and Barnabas hadn't sent ten men to their deaths—rather, they had saved ten from jumping from the President Kennedy Bridge near the bar where they drank. Only after police, firefighters, paramedics, psychiatrists, psychologists and even spiritual leaders failed would they leap into action.

They were drunk and disorderly, but they understood the finer points of emotional peaks and valleys. They knew that psychological jargon had little effect on someone who had condemned himself to death. My friends taunted the victim to make him project his anger onto them.

It moved me profoundly. Although I had known depression in the past, I was still an empty intellectual, a coward, an insensitive thinker who detested compromising his image by turning to others for help. As the dreamseller said, we're all experts at hiding things.

The young boxer was still drunk with rage. He struggled to break free to continue beating them.

"Why would you hit someone who saved your life?" I told him. "Why would you punch someone who gave of himself and loved you without knowing you?"

My voice was so strident that he stopped in his tracks. The crowd fell silent. I continued:

"Don't you realize they provoked your anger on purpose? Don't you understand that they made you hate them so you wouldn't hate yourself? They wouldn't let you use a period to end your life. They sold you a comma so you could go on writing your story."

The young man's anger cooled as my words washed over him. His name was Felipe, but people called him "Crusher" in the ring. He had always dealt violently with his opponents, until he was knocked out by events in his life. Sooner or later everyone is KO'd in life, but Felipe never accepted his defeat. A man who had always been violent with others could act no differently with himself.

The boxer came to his senses and concluded that the two agitators had served as sparring partners—without using any protective gear.

He looked at the two men. Bartholomew had a dark ring forming around his left eye and was bleeding from a cut just above it. The Mayor's lips were swollen and he was bleeding from the right side of his mouth.

The young man collapsed and started crying unabashedly, with no fear of the audience, no fear of criticism, no fear of his own feelings. The onlookers fell totally silent. Each teardrop spoke to the young man's pain.

It was just as the dreamseller had told us: Each person has his reasons for crumbling. Life is cyclical and there are no heroes who can be on top forever. Every person has his reasons for crying—some tears we see, while others are hidden from sight. Crusher had his own demons, and they were many. But he left behind a world of self-destruction to enter our world of sublime kindness.

He got up from his knees and hugged Honeymouth and the Mayor with uncommon affection. Bartholomew and Barnabas, who hadn't any family until they found us, melted in light of such caring. Crusher brought his chest up against theirs. He thought nothing could keep him from killing himself, but then he had met two lunatics so in love with life that they torpedoed his plans.

All three were crying. Tears and blood mixed like ink to write a new story. It was the first time I'd seen men who were strangers cry and embrace like that, a phenomenon not found in psychology texts but one described in the dreamseller's manual.

Crusher then turned to hug Professor Jurema and kissed her on the cheek. "Thanks for the spanking, Granny."

She, too, had tears in her eyes. On days like this, she felt it was easy to follow the Dreamseller. She had once shined in the classroom. And now, as her days to pass on new lessons out in the world became fewer, she shined at selling dreams.

Bartholomew and Barnabas had taken real beatings when they used this strategy to convince jumpers to get down from the bridge. The price they paid was high. Twice they had to stay in the hospital. They had bones broken three times.

After Crusher had asked their forgiveness, it was my turn to do the same.

"I'm sorry for misjudging you," I said.

This time Honeymouth spared me. "I might have done the same thing in your place." Turning to Crusher, he said, "I'm sorry for pissing you off. I was already buried under the banks, but you almost sent me to the cemetery."

We all laughed. The Mayor interjected, "You rearranged my face, dude. I won't be able to chew for an hour."

The tension had dissipated and Crusher felt comfortable enough to tell us about the problems that had sent him to the top of that monument.

"I'm a professional boxer. I was suspended for six months for using a medication they considered 'performance enhancing.' They killed me in the press. My father, my best friend, died of a heart attack two months later. I was a week from getting married, when I lost my shirt in the stock market. I lost my money and my fiancée."

That's when the dreamseller walked up to us. He had been watching from a distance, allowing his anonymous disciples to act on their own. "My son, we all have forty-six chromosomes in our cells, but we're all very different in how we handle adversity. There's no such thing as a sky without storms." What he said next shook the disciples, especially me. "I once stood on a bridge, at the height of my despair. I didn't want to die, but I had no spirit to go on living. But then, I ran into two young drop-down drunks. They provoked and insulted me. They were relentless. I half expected them to toss their whiskey in my face."

Bartholomew and Barnabas couldn't believe it. They didn't know the dreamseller was one of the people they had rescued. Because they were drunk most of the time, they couldn't remember much at all about who they had rescued. I was stupefied and I wondered, "Could these two have shaped the dreamseller's desire to sell dreams? Can the pupil teach the master? Can the patient cure the doctor?"

"After that shock, I went into hiding and spent a lot of time rethinking my life. That was when I came to understand that frustrations are a privilege of the living and transcending them is a privilege of the wise," said the dreamseller.

A few people in the crowd wrote down that sentiment. And then the dreamseller began to applaud Felipe, Bartholomew, Barnabas and Jurema. Soon, the entire crowd was clapping. However, applause is a dangerous thing for the Mayor. Although he was injured, he leaned on the person nearest him and launched into a short speech

"Thank you very much, my splendid and abyssal public," he said in a slurred voice, as if he were drunk. "Vote for me in the coming election." By this point, three people were holding up his mammoth frame.

"What office are you running for?" asked a crowd member who realized there were no upcoming elections.

Honeymouth answered for him. "Chief lunatic of this global insane asylum," he said, gesturing all around him.

They all broke out laughing, even Crusher. He got the message. He was one more inmate learning to laugh at his own madness. "You've got my vote," he cheered.

The dreamseller seconded his vote.

The people around them all pledged their votes. Inspired, the dreamseller looked Crusher in the eye and invited him to become a follower. Honeymouth looked approvingly at Barnabas and said, "I'll be your secretary of finance, brother."

"Anything but finance, you old pickpocket!"

"How can you say that, Mayor? I'm an upstanding citizen now," Bartholomew said. But, he turned to the dreamseller and asked him for forgiveness for his life before they met: "Master, before I met you, I thought there was a chance I wasn't a saint. Today . . . well, today I'm sure I'm not."

None of us were saints. We all understood that. And although the dreamseller and those two knuckleheads might not change our insane asylum of a world, we knew they could make it a fun place to live.

We left hugging one another, leaving behind a crowd of

more than a hundred people looking for a taste of adventure.
As we departed, we sang our song:

I'm just a wanderer
Who lost the fear of getting lost,
Certain of his own imperfection;
You may say I'm crazy
You may mock my ideas
It doesn't matter!
What matters is I'm a wanderer,
Who sells dreams to passersby;
I've no compass or schedule,
I have nothing, yet I have everything.
I'm just a wanderer
In search of myself.

CHAPTER 14

Unusual Leaders

D AYS LATER, A WINDSWEPT FLYER LANDED AGAINST THE
dreamseller's chest. He read that a Leaders of the Future
seminar was to be held that night, and he decided to participate.
Since the event was sponsored by the Megasoft Foundation
and admission was free, we were confident we could get in.
However, as always, our ratty clothes made us a target for the
security guards.

People of all ages and nationalities entered without a problem, but vagrants were once again kept out. The security guards
checked us from head to toe, asking us to spread our arms and
scanned us for guns, bombs and dangerous chemical products.

"Very generous of those guys. I enjoyed the free massage,"
the Mayor said.

We took our seats in the center of the amphitheater, in the
thirteenth row. We were about fifty feet from the speakers,
who spoke about the molding of political, business and institu-
tional leaders who would change the future of humanity.

The Mayor and Honeymouth sat next to each other. In
less than fifteen minutes they were sound asleep. The rest of
the crew was barely able to keep their eyes open. Some of the
speakers were so technical and monotonous. Obviously, it was
too much to ask that the dreamseller's followers develop a taste

for this since they had never been taught to develop a taste for the fare of the academic world.

I never understood how the Mayor and Honeymouth, who loved to cause a scene, could always keep such sound minds. They managed to fall asleep effortlessly. I remembered reading an article that said that major business leaders relied on pills to sleep. Without their tranquilizers, their minds were restless.

The Mayor's snoring was as loud as a dissonant orchestra, the noise thundering five rows in all directions. Even the speakers looked to see what all the racket was about. I kept nudging the Mayor to quiet his snoring.

But the Mayor was on cloud nine, dreaming he was swimming in a pot of spaghetti *al sugo*. He mumbled, "delicious . . . tasty . . . delectable." The spectators in front of us started turning around. I stuffed a handkerchief in his mouth. He started chewing on it and soon calmed down.

Honeymouth was so relaxed that he began dreaming he was floating through the clouds, riding a winged horse. Making small hand movements to control the animal, he touched the heads of those in the next row. Monica, Jurema, and I tried to keep his hands to himself.

"If we depend on these two," I thought, "humanity is in for a dark future."

Soon, though, they quieted down and we were able to listen to the lecture series. During the final address, Bartholomew and Barnabas began dreaming simultaneously that they were fighting each other over a beautiful woman. It was a familiar dream, which often caused us problems under the bridges and in the shelters where we slept.

At the exact moment when they imagined they were vying for the princess's hand, the event's final speech began, dealing with great leaders of the past and their fundamental characteristics. The speaker mentioned the self-confidence, determination, concentration, focus and transparency of King Solomon, Napoleon, Henry Ford, Thomas Edison, John F. Kennedy and others.

Just as the lecturer spoke about the leaders, Bartholomew and Barnabas, lost in their dreams, shouted, "Scoundrel! Rogue! I'm gonna rip your heart out!" People thought they were being critical of the lecturer and shouted them down. It was all we could do to keep them quiet.

Suddenly, they started caressing each other's heads, imagining they had finally reached the princess. And that was when the panic ensued. They opened their eyes, stared at each other and screamed.

"Help!" they shouted simultaneously, as if they'd seen a ghost. The lecturer and other participants thought the building was on fire. The lecturer interrupted his speech and I sank down in my seat, trying to make myself invisible.

The room was a veritable summit of political and social heavy hitters from around the world. The organizer of the event, along with three security men, came to investigate the source of the disturbance. When he approached, he saw me with my head down, as if I were responsible. He asked me to look up, which I did reluctantly. Startled, he recognized me.

"Julio Cesar?"

It was Tulio de Campos, a colleague from the university. Tulio was a professor I had frequently criticized when I was chairman of the sociology department. His ego was as big as mine, and equal egos repel. We couldn't stand each other. Having heard that I was wandering the streets with a strange man, he took his revenge. He humiliated me in public, calling me irresponsible, a rabble-rouser, a cut-rate intellectual. He tore me down just as I had done to him a little more than two years earlier.

"Everyone knows you went crazy, Julio Cesar. And now you're trying to undermine my work?"

"It's true. The guy's nuts. But he's a good man," Honey-mouth, said, humiliating me even more.

"So this is your group of bedlamites, eh? Why don't you spare us all the headache and get out of here," Tulio said.

"What's going on, here?" the Mayor asked. "We're nuts, crazies, weirdos, but not bedla—bedla—bedlamites!" Then he gestured to Professor Jurema for help with the meaning of the word.

"Bedlamite," she explained, "means insane, unhinged, a lunatic."

"Oh, gooood! Then he got it right." And he gave Tulio a thumbs-up, irritating him even more.

The dreamseller raised his right hand to speak.

"Sir, these men are not perfect, but each is brilliant in his own way, just as you are clearly a great leader as the organizer of this event. And a great leader, in order not to have a heart attack at an early age, must possess, among other qualities, two in particular: good humor and tolerance. Good humor to avoid stressing at one's own stupidity and tolerance to avoid stressing at the stupidity of others."

Tulio reeled. He realized for a few seconds that he was both punitive and self-loathing, neither tolerant nor good-humored. But, raising a finger, he stated in an authoritative tone, "Any more noise and you'll be immediately removed."

My mouth was filled with the bitter taste of humiliation. I had never allowed anyone to speak to me with such self-importance. I had fired five professors after minor confrontations. Now the shoe was on the other foot, and it hurt. It was tough seeing myself reflected in Tulio.

The lecture resumed, but the speaker had gone off the rails. Like many lecturers, he could only speak brilliantly if everything worked flawlessly. He stumbled on and mercifully brought an end to the event's final presentation.

A Megasoft executive thanked everyone for their participation, adding "except for some," while clearing his throat. He praised the conglomerate to which he belonged, stating that its focus was investment in shaping human beings, and in the rights of citizens and the promotion of society's well being. And he concluded by saying that this seminar would help change the course of history.

After the applause died down, I thought we might leave without further disruption, but the dreamseller rose from his seat and brandished some words that woke up the more than two hundred people present. As he began to speak, the house lights came back up.

"How can we shape future leaders without reforming our educational system? A society that pays its judges many times what it pays its teachers will always face major difficulties in creating great leaders. Our system is sick, turning out sick people for a sick society. What kind of future awaits us?"

The audience was surprised at the audacity of this shabbily dressed man. Who was this man? Was he trying to restart the seminar? In a way, he was. Some wondered who he was. Others recognized him immediately and began spreading the word that he was the wanderer who had been taking the city by storm.

CHAPTER 15

Newspapers: A Source of Nourishment

THE DREAMSELLER FOCUSED ON THE IMPORTANCE OF molding young leaders, something that worried him greatly, since it would one day be their task to take on humanity's problems.

"Our young are not feeding their minds with the intellectual diet capable of providing the nutrients they need: critical awareness and the development of their role as social activists." What he said next went to the heart of my prejudices as a college professor. Their minds should not be built in the classroom, he said, but through newspapers.

"Free and independent newspapers currently represent the major source of intellectual nourishment for the human mind. But young people have neither easy access to them or interest in reading them. Editors, reporters, columnists organize their minds daily to shape a newspaper. To me, newspapers are as important—or more important—than books. But they're dying. The ritual of leafing through a newspaper, the pleasure of informing oneself and diving into the information sweeping across the nation is a delight. But new technologies, spearheaded by the Internet, are strangling that delight. How will we form new leaders if the young spend hours a day watching TV or surfing for entertainment sites and don't spend even a

minute a week informing themselves about the political, social and economic facts that permeate the globalized world? We
won't form leaders but slaves."

I was impressed. I've always talked about critical thinking,
but I never imagined that the dreamseller thought newspapers contributed more to such thinking than outdated school
curriculums. Now I know why the he read them late into the
night and encouraged his disciples to read them, even if they
were two or three days old. Now I understand why my uncultured and noisy partners were enriching their brains. And the
dreamseller commented on another aberration of the system.

"It's a crime against education for students to spend years
studying a tiny atom they'll never see and an immense outer
space they'll never tread and yet not spend time getting to
know the world inside them. They must learn how thought is
formed and how thinkers are formed, how to act upon their
mind and how to act in society."

The audience broke into applause. Suddenly, no one wanted
to leave. They wanted to stay to hear this intriguing and controversial prophet, the street thinker.

"To those who would be leaders, I recommend they spend
time getting to know what is in the mind of the anonymous.
Politicians should bow down to their most humble of voters.
Psychiatrists should learn from the mentally ill. Intellectuals
should be taught through the imagination of the illiterate. And
celebrities? They should cede the spotlight to the unknowns.
Train yourselves to see the world through the eyes of others."

He let his words hang in the air, preferring to let people
think and draw their own conclusions. But the audience went
from applause to scorn in less than a minute. They broke into
laughter, thinking it was a joke to lighten the mood. After all,
since the time of the Greeks and Romans the lesser members
of society were always led, controlled and subjugated by the

more powerful. It would be counterintuitive to bow to their inferiors.

In modern society, our beliefs hadn't changed but had merely taken on new trappings. The blood rushed to my cheeks when I heard the laughter around me. I was hoping the dreamseller wouldn't expand on his thinking, but then his disciples raised their voices to echo his thoughts. Again, I wished I were invisible.

"Dreamseller, I've always thought that celebrities should bow down before us," Bartholomew said, pointing to us. I tried to hide my face. "It's finally our time, the time of the underprivileged, the poor, the nobodies. Let's revolt and show society our strength in numbers!"

Suddenly, the Mayor sprang into action. "Yes, the revolution of the bedlamites, the crazies, the lunatics, the unhinged," the Mayor said, puffing out his chest. "I've always thought psychiatrists should learn from my noteworthy ideas."

I tried to cover his mouth to keep him from uttering more nonsense, but he was standing up. I refused to be a part of that ignoble band of revolutionaries. These eccentrics hadn't understood a single word about the dreamseller's revolution. Hadn't understood that he had chosen us, the craziest of society, to shame the sages and make the leaders blush.

"Yes, it's the time of con men and scam artists," Dimas said then quickly caught himself: "I mean *recovering* con men."

"And the time of the obsessive-compulsives and the hypochondriacs," Solomon yelled.

"Hallelujah! It's the time for the faithful to display their miracles," Edson added.

If I were the dreamseller, I might have run from their delusions, but he listened to them patiently. But in the back of my mind, a voice was telling me that I was as sick as anyone in this world-wide insane asylum. Suddenly, beautiful Monica, the first female disciple to follow the dreamseller, spoke up.

"Yes, it's time for women who aren't in the fashion magazines, who have been swept aside by the media because they don't measure up to the dictatorial standard of beauty," she said. Monica proclaimed these words as if she were Joan of Arc trying to liberate women from the tyrannical yoke of thinness imposed by the leaders of the fashion world. Monica knew what she was talking about; she had been one of the most sought-after international models until she was discarded after gaining a few pounds.

"Yes! And it's time for the elderly to bombard society with Factor E!" said Professor Jurema. "You young people," she continued, "are shiftless, lazy, fragile, spoiled, timid, and narrow-minded. You're like gravediggers watching over the dead. You talk a lot but don't act." And she said nothing more. She didn't have to.

"Factor E for empty-headed. The old lady's batty," a young student muttered under his breath.

Suddenly, she thumped him on the head with her cane. "E for experience," she said. "Knowledge without experience is useless."

Only Crusher and I didn't speak up. Though very strong, he remained silent, for fear of being lynched. I felt embarrassed, spewing an opinion in a place where I hadn't been invited.

Without another word, the dreamseller left, and we quickly followed him. The audience stayed behind for a few moments thinking about all that had been said, digesting our ideas. But some of them were clearly experiencing heartburn.

A few blocks away, the dreamseller called me aside. He was an expert at correcting in private and praising in public, never the other way around. "What's bothering you, Julio Cesar?"

"Master, your disciples just don't grasp your philosophy."

"They grasp it within their limits. Why not respect those limits?"

"They bring shame down on you, and they can destroy your image, destroy your plan for selling dreams. It's because of them that people don't know how to define you, as either a wise man or a lunatic."

Like a father correcting his son, he told me, "I've learned to accept being cheered and being booed, being loved and hated, being understood and defamed. What will I take away when the breath of life ceases? No slander can tear away a shred of my being, unless I allow it. Ideas are seeds, and the greatest favor that can ever happen to a seed is for it to be buried. A man without friends is soil without water, a morning without dew, a sky without clouds. Friends are not those who flatter us but those who demystify us and expose our vulnerability. An intellectual without friends is a book without words."

I had to admit that I had had admirers, but I was a man without friends. I neither had anyone to whom I lent a shoulder to cry on, nor had I had ever lent a shoulder. My ego was too big, my pride enormous, but my solidarity was minuscule. I was a man of contradictions.

Over the years, students asked me to act as their mentor for their master's and doctoral theses, but we never plumbed the depths of our personality. Three university students tried to commit suicide the last year I taught. Ten students suffered depression. Several dozen had psychosomatic illnesses. But I never went to visit them. A professor and his students were miles apart.

We couldn't appreciate how to formulate thoughts or thinkers. I was sick and shaping sick people for a sick society. I pretended to teach, and they pretended to learn. And diplomas justified our playacting.

CHAPTER 16

The Intelligent Poor

M ANY YOUNG PEOPLE FOLLOWED FADS FOR HOW TO DRESS, talk and behave. To be different from the group caused them anxiety. They lacked a style of their own and were controlled by marketing that permeated every fiber of the fabric of society. Some young people not only followed fads but also rejected anyone who didn't fit into the shortsighted view of the world. They detested the very idea of homosexuals, beggars and other minorities.

Five days after the uproar at the leadership conference, a significant event occurred. The dreamseller had left his disciples on their own as he went looking for a calm setting in which to meditate. To the dreamseller, solitude was an invitation to know himself and embark into the universe of reflection.

A group of about fifteen upper-middle- and upper-class university students began to taunt us when they saw Dimas, Edson, Bartholomew, Barnabas and me in our old patched clothes. The group thought homeless people were a blight on society, a problem worthy of violence.

As they passed by us, one of them stuck out his left foot out and tripped the Mayor, who fell like a ton of bricks. We rushed to help him, but he wasn't injured. We thought it was an accident, but then I noticed they were laughing as one of them said,

"Check out the dregs of society!" We stopped and faced each other. They seemed to be aching for a fight. My nerves were on edge. My instincts as a professor took over and I shouted without thinking, "Get out of my classroom!"

Seeing me act like a crazed professor, they burst out laughing. For the first time in my life, I was humiliated by students.

One of them went further. He walked toward me and yelled, "Get a load of the master of morons!"

Instead of being intimidated, Bartholomew thrust out his chest and said, "Behold the future of society: youngsters who live in their daddy's shadow, who have never fallen but want to lift up the world!" And *he* broke out laughing.

The students hated his cockiness. Some were ready to pounce on him. One of them retorted, "The destiny of great leaders is to rid society of its trash."

The Mayor suddenly injected himself into the scene. "Vote for me in the next election and I'll spare you."

The youths thought they were being ridiculed. They were puzzled by the boldness of this group of ragamuffins. They didn't know anything about the dreamseller who had trained us.

Crusher was enraged. Just as some of the youths were getting ready to confront us physically, I proposed a change in the field of battle:

"Why not fight in the realm of ideas? If you can answer a few questions right, we'll let you kick our butts. If you can't answer, we get to kick yours."

They thought it would be like taking candy from a baby.

"It's a deal. Bring on the questions."

I took a deep breath and began the quiz.

"Who was Immanuel Kant? What was Montaigne's central line of thought? Can you tell us about the accomplishments of Spinoza?"

They took a step back, not knowing how to answer. They whispered among themselves, "Where did these guys get those names?" Seeing their confusion, I started hammering them.

"Do you know the history of the Phoenicians, the Hebrews, the Persians? The Minoan world? The Mycenaean culture, the Homeric period?"

The students were flabbergasted. They looked at each other in a cold sweat. They never expected homeless people to have brains, much less working ones that could leave them speechless.

Outside of their required reading in school, many of them read almost nothing.

They were the Harry Potter generation, the generation of instant gratification who wanted everything as if by magic. Like high-ranking military officers, they demanded that their parents be their servants. They were skilled at complaining but terrible at expressing gratitude. They lacked the will, the ambition, the ability to compete and survive in the world. They used the Internet, but their culture was as shallow as a puddle of water. They had nothing but disdain for history and philosophy, ignorant to the fact that to see the future it was necessary to study the past.

Suddenly, Dimas, the confidence man of the group, jumped in.

"Why did the world's stock markets collapse? Do you know what a subprime mortgage is?" We all followed a man who, though very poor, read a lot. Watching the dreamseller devour newspapers and magazines, his uncultured disciples eventually developed a taste for reading. A few days earlier I had seen Dimas buried in the business section of the newspaper.

Edson, the group's theologian, added, "Do any of you have any idea what the Gaza Strip is?"

After some thought, one of the youths ventured, "Is that some kind of pizza?"

Then the Mayor summed it up. "You'll forgive me, my young friends, but it seems you're in the world but from some other world."

"I like that, Mayor," Honeymouth said. "They're aliens making fun of aliens. Well, it's time to pay off the bet, kids. Turn around."

The students began backing away, holding their hands over their butts. But Honeymouth, remembering the dreamseller, said, "Don't worry, we're not gonna kick you. Only the weak use force. The strong use ideas. The future of the world depends on you and not on us vagabonds. It was an honor to meet you."

We waved to the young men and sent them on their way. They were rich, we were poor, but we possessed something that couldn't be bought or sold. The students left wordlessly and quickly dispersed. The students wouldn't sleep that night. Some reconsidered their role in society and began to buy the dream of critical thinking. They began to see beyond the limits of images.

All these experiences led me to discoveries that disconcerted me. I came to understand that it was not only particular groups of young people who were prejudiced and exclusionary but also some groups of intellectuals, especially the radical followers of certain ideologies: like all the "ians," like the Piagetians, or the "ists."

I belonged to the "ists." I was a rabid socialist and saw little benefit of other social theories. Only after I began following the dreamseller and living with that controversial group of friends did I expand my mind and break down barriers. I've been learning that the worst enemies of any theory are those who most radically adhere to it, who don't have the courage to see beyond it.

I was an expert in the ideas of Marx, Engel, Hegel and Lenin but did very little to change the society I lived in—or to change myself. I prepared students to be good test takers but not to debate ideas. I didn't care whether they were creative or slaves to trends. I was a rigid professor criticizing a rigid society.

I didn't stimulate my students to delve into history or philosophy, to go beyond the boundaries of my subject. I was one of the gravediggers who helped to bury their imagination and sensitivity. I did nothing to prevent the formation of psychopaths. After all, some psychopaths have high IQs.

One of the dreamseller's teachings, which cut like a razor, was that any debt can be repaid, or set aside, except the debt of conscience: *whoever is not faithful to his conscience has an unpayable debt to himself.*

I'm learning to pay off debts to my conscience. It's not easy to recognize my immaturity and talk about what I'm ashamed of. But to flee from myself is to perpetuate my misfortunes and to take my problems with me to an early grave.

CHAPTER 17

Flying on a Chicken Wing

WE WERE WALKING THROUGH A POOR DISTRICT IN THE South Zone. The dreamseller loved to go there, where he had several friends who were manual laborers, machine operators, drivers, custodians, and some were unemployed. What they lacked in resources, they made up for in feelings. They gladly shared what little they had.

Sometimes they would invite us to lunch or dinner. The dreamseller was particularly fond of Luiz Lemos, though we didn't know him. Later we learned that he was a man who had suffered, but was happy, balanced and above all uncomplicated. A paraplegic, he had lost the use of his legs in an automobile accident. He was married to Mercedes, a helpful and lively woman though she had only one leg, having lost the other in an accident at work.

The couple had no children of their own but looked after the children of others, despite their limitations. The dreamseller had been in their house before and they loved having him. He and Luiz Lemos appeared to be longtime friends.

Once, the couple invited the entire group to have lunch at their house. Since the house was small, without a yard and with only a tiny living room—between seventy and eighty square feet—this lunch was not for the crowds, but only for the inner circle of disciples.

We took the subway and, after changing lines twice and passing through more than ten stations, we arrived at the Corujas neighborhood where the couple lived. We left the subway and set off on foot to their house. After climbing a steep hill and making several turns, our tongues were hanging out by the time we arrived at their home twenty minutes later.

"Wow, we're really earning our lunch today," the Mayor said, exhausted. His corpulent body wasn't up to physical exertion. He preferred his food to come to him.

Honeymouth, seeing the humble neighborhood where the Lemos family resided, commented good-naturedly, "I can't get over how many poor people there are in the world. Still, I prefer living in our Kennedy mansion." He was referring to our bridge.

Luiz Lemos was a millionaire compared to us. We were paupers, with neither a living room, bedroom or sofa, much less an armoire. To follow the dreamseller meant adhering to a certain lifestyle. Besides learning to recognize our stupidity and inconsistency, we lived with only just enough money to make it through the day. People rightly considered us less fortunate, homeless, hopeless and godforsaken. We slept under the blue star-studded blanket. Luckily, a few doctors carried blankets in the trunks of their cars and on cold nights would distribute them.

The well-off disciples would sleep at home and in the morning try to find us. But because the dreamseller followed no set schedule they weren't always successful. Monica and Jurema were among those who lived like "normals," but they were nevertheless two of the most tireless "abnormals." And they were with us that day.

Our hosts' house was not glamorous. Cracked, peeling walls.

Windows with faded paint and rusted sides. A leaky roof that
was rotted through. In the living room was a table with four
chairs. The couple barely fit into the cramped space.

As we approached Luiz Lemos's house we saw him eagerly
awaiting us in his wheelchair. From ten yards away, the dreamseller was already shouting hello:

"My good friend Luiz Lemos! And how is the man who
travels freely where others dare not tread?" They hugged and
kissed each other's cheeks.

With uncommon reverence, Lemos replied, "I'm unworthy
of having you in my home."

The dreamseller answered, "I'm the one who's unworthy
to enter your home." Then he placed his hands on Mercedes's
shoulders and asked her, "And how is this enchanting woman?"
He hugged her and kissed her delicately on the forehead.

"What an honor to have you in our humble home," they
told us as if receiving a king and his princes.

We greeted them warmly. The dreamseller chatted pleas-
antly with the couple about the latest happenings in his life.
Minutes later, the Mayor's CES (compulsive eating syndrome)
began to affect his brain. Impatient and starved, and without a
spare sandwich in his pocket, his shameless politician persona
manifested itself:

"Honorable hosts of this hungry tribe: Are we here to talk
or to eat?"

"To talk!" Monica and Jurema said, trying to gloss over his
rudeness.

"To eat!" Honeymouth, Dimas, Solomon and Edson said simultaneously and loudly. I wanted to crawl into a hole but, as
always, straddled the fence. I was hungry, too, but I preferred
to politely disguise my grumbling stomach.

Mercedes, having heard of the dreamseller's imps, said,
"Let's eat before the food gets cold."

She had prepared a small roasted chicken, a stew, a green salad and generous servings of white rice. She was an excellent cook.

Given the extremely tight space, at the host's suggestion we moved the table to the bedroom and sat on the living room floor.

"I propose," said Bartholomew, trying to bring order to the chaos, "that we form a line and serve ourselves in the kitchen and sit in this magnificent living room."

And to show his fine manners, he added, "Mercedes and Mr. Luiz Lemos will be the first served."

The host and hostess naturally declined the offer. "Please," Luiz Lemos said, "you first."

That was when I caught on to his scheme. Bartholomew and Barnabas were strategically placed at the kitchen door in order to be the first to serve themselves. I was outraged by their gall, but the dreamseller seemed amused. He was in heaven. To him, everything was a party.

The two wise guys, like soldiers in a war, attacked the chicken, heading straight for the drumsticks and even tearing off a chunk of the breast. To disguise the stratagem, they buried their pieces of chicken under a mountain of rice.

Then Solomon, Edson and Dimas served themselves. They tore into what remained of the breast and ripped it apart. They gave no thought to me, despite knowing I loved roast chicken. Crusher also served himself, though awkwardly. When my turn came, only the mortal remains of the blessed bird were to be seen. Not even the neck had survived. Crusher took one wing and I took the other. The Master had salad and a few pieces of meat. Monica and Jurema did the same.

The two sly foxes waited anxiously for everyone to serve themselves so we could start the meal together, a practice of the dreamseller's. We all sat down, squeezed in like sardines.

Edson was so famished that he didn't even say grace; he merely looked up, down and tore into his food. Solomon and Dimas didn't even blink; they only made time for swallowing. The dreamseller silently gave thanks for the food that nourished him.

Bartholomew and Barnabas ate like barbarians. Suddenly, Honeymouth stopped chewing. With his full mouth, he said, "Hold up, people. Let's thank those who prepared the food." I found his sudden altruism strange.

Everyone stopped eating. We had to quickly swallow the juicy bite that brought joy to our salivary glands. Honeymouth was so euphoric with his piece of chicken that he said:

"Mercedes and Mr. Luiz Lemos, thank you very much for inviting us, I hope not for the last time." Then he had the gall to ask all present to spear the chicken on their forks and raise it to the sky.

I wanted to hide my face in shame, but I followed his lead because I didn't want to look like a spoilsport. He and Barnabas were like two generals carrying their most highly prized spoils of war, firmly and proudly clutching their drumsticks.

I, on the contrary, felt like the conquered, holding up my bony, puny wing. Crusher raised his sad wing, as well. We looked at each other and shook our heads.

I lost my appetite. I felt that even when they expressed their gratitude these two scoundrels were needling me and showing that my intellectuality was worthless. Once again I discovered that intellectuals are no match for street smarts. Subtly, they dominated businesses, universities, politics and even life under bridges, while we spent so much time thinking.

"Lord, forgive me for my covetousness and thank you for this spectacular poultry," he said, trying to excuse himself.

And to sour my appetite even more, the Mayor added,

"Amen! May the chickens of the earth multiply, and peace fill the hearts of the shrewd and the gullible."

Mercedes and her husband were amused by the pair. This time I couldn't ignore the provocation. I turned to the Master and said, "Dreamseller, these two are calling me gullible, an ignoramus."

"Julio Cesar, my hope for all of you is that you may order a taste of tranquillity from the menu of existence. When the intellect is free, food takes on another flavor. A simple meal eaten in peace is better than the finest dishes eaten amid anguish and anger."

I fell silent before the dreamseller's wisdom, but Honeymouth, with his unstoppable capacity for talking, spewed forth like a street philosopher.

"Master, to build on your theory, I'd like to say that Julio Cesar can go further with legs than with his tiny wings . . ."

The Mayor, Dimas and Solomon congratulated him. "Thank you, but I'm merely an emerging genius," he said with false modesty.

And without further delay, they devoured their food. Traveling with Bartholomew and Barnabas, I don't know whether I was training to be humble or training to meet the monsters of rage and indignation buried in my story. I had to learn either to react less to their provocations and make life a party or else I would have a heart attack.

Just as I was promising myself I'd never again eat a chicken wing, I remembered scream therapy and bellowed, "Aaaahhh! Uuuhhh!"

Bartholomew and the Mayor were so startled that they dropped their drumsticks on the floor, only to pick them up again, sheepishly. They'd had a taste of their own medicine.

I burst out laughing. My friends, especially Monica and

Jurema, were impressed with me. I had never acted like that. For the first time, I felt good about playing the clown. I understood that smiling at our idiotic behavior is a miraculous cure for a bad mood. I apologized to our host then went back to eating, happy as a lark.

The dreamseller didn't scold me. In fact, he nodded his head in satisfaction. He realized I was beginning to learn how to savor my meals.

CHAPTER 18

An Assassination Attempt on the Dreamseller

After eating and talking for a while, we said goodbye to the friendly Luiz Lemos and Mercedes. The dreamseller hugged them affectionately. I had never seen people who did so much with so little. Giving of themselves is what nourished their emotional needs. Honeymouth asked for forgiveness, but not for himself. Rather, for the rest of us, me in particular.

"Excuse my friends if they didn't behave well. But in a few decades the dreamseller will change them. Please, every time you prepare a chicken, remember this hungry mouth."

Bartholomew never lost his sense of humor.

Just as the Mayor was about to open his mouth to babble something, I told him, "Save your breath, it's a long way home."

Fortunately, recalling his fatigue, he listened: "Thank you, my chief of staff, for taking care of me."

The way down was truly grueling. We tried a short cut and ended up in a street barely wide enough for a car. Three blocks down, we turned to the left and found ourselves in a dead end. As we tried to retrace our steps, we found our path blocked by five heavy-set, rough-looking men. We hadn't noticed that they were following us. As they came closer, people in the vicinity began closing their windows and doors.

A chill ran down our backs. We knew we were in real danger. When they drew within forty yards of us, they put on hoods. They moved faster. At ten yards away they took revolvers and a pair of machine guns from their long coats. We were dead. I was sure of it.

Three of the criminals were white. The fourth was black, not tall but extremely muscular. The fifth was short, but agile and calculating; he looked as if he had come from the dungeons of the Chinese mafia. He was the leader of the group, and it made me shudder to look at him. From his quick movements, he appeared to be a master in martial arts.

"Freeze!" they ordered, pointing their guns at us. I became dizzy. I had never been in a high-risk situation. Crusher's lips started trembling. Monica and Jurema burst into tears. Edson's voice faltered. Solomon experienced a panic attack.

The Asian man became more violent and merciless as we withered.

"Dead men don't cry. So shut your mouths!" He took a photo from his pocket, looked at the dreamseller and compared the images.

Glancing at his companions, he nodded, confirming that this was the one they were after. They pointed their weapons at the dreamseller and at us. The dreamseller, who seemed to know he would die sooner or later and had no fear of saying farewell to life, told them in a firm voice:

"Even a killer has to have some dignity when he carries a gun. If you want my life, why shed innocent blood? Let the others go," he told his executioners.

Hearing this, the killers were motionless for several seconds. Then, surprisingly, the dreamseller took control and shouted to us, "Leave! Now!"

We all ran, expecting to hear gunshots hot on our trail. The elderly Jurema and Monica ran like rabbits. Dimas leaped like a leopard. Edson appeared to have sprouted wings. Solomon forgot he was having a coronary and darted. Crusher and I had never run so fast in our lives. But the shots didn't come.

We rounded the corner and continued to flee. A couple of hundred yards from the scene, we stopped briefly to catch our breath. Two of the disciples were missing: Bartholomew and Barnabas. We waited for them, but they had stayed behind. Stayed behind to die with the dreamseller. Stayed behind to be at the side of one they loved. Stayed behind because the dreamseller was all they had. I couldn't believe their heroism.

We wanted desperately to get out of that labyrinth and find the police. But the police station seemed a long way off. We asked several people for help, but they were afraid for their lives. We went on as fast as we could, but we knew it was hopeless. The execution would be swift.

Exhausted, I stopped. I began to cry. I couldn't accept the idea of the dreamseller being summarily executed. The man who saved my life and made me love life would be cut down mercilessly. As he said, "We present our story like eternal players in the theater of time and suddenly end the play as if we had never acted." I felt miserable, guilty for having done nothing for the man who had done so much for me.

The disciples who gave him the most problems were also the most loyal. I began to feel sad at the thought of participating in the wake for Bartholomew and Barnabas. I couldn't imagine life without their humor and antics. Yes, they tormented me, but they also brought color to my tedious and suffocating existence. I never imagined they would become a part of me.

While my friends and I cried like children, the assassins were preparing to carry out their mission. They pointed their guns at the three men, who didn't stand a chance. As they were about to pull the trigger, the Mayor spoke.

"One moment, sir. Let me say my last words," he told their

leader, who stood immobile in surprise. "Thank you, kind assassin." Turning his head, he said, "Dreamseller, you embraced me, believed in me, and invested your attention in me. You were more than a father. It is an honor to die at your side. Honeymouth, you were a pain for many years, but you were my brother." Then he dried his tears and made a request to his murderers: "You can kill me, but bury us both in the same coffin."

Hearing this, Honeymouth forgot he was at gunpoint and found the energy for one last confrontation with Barnabas:

"Easy there, Mayor. Not together! It was hard enough putting up with you in *this* life." And, looking at his killers, he uttered not a request but an order: "Go ahead and shoot, but I demand a coffin all my own."

The killers had never encountered victims who behaved like that. They wanted to concentrate on their job but kept wondering, "Just who the heck are these guys?"

When they were about to fire, it was the dreamseller's turn to intervene.

"I don't believe these jerks are going to kill us without amusing themselves," he said, defiantly. And he began jumping around like a clown, trying to imitate a martial arts expert. He tripped over his own feet and fell.

The hit men snorted. Just a few days ago, Bartholomew and Barnabas had seen the dreamseller disarm a man who was going to shoot him at point-blank range. They now wondered whether it as a fluke.

Still, Bartholomew took heart at seeing him challenge the criminals to a fight.

"They're five losers." And turning his back on their leader, he said provocatively, "And the little one there looks like a pansy! Just 'cause he's got a machine gun he thinks he's a tough guy." And he broke into laughter.

The executioners were used to killing but they had never

seen three people ready to meet their end so sarcastically, mocking them, even being abusive and cocky. The leader became embroiled in a fit of rage, ready to abandon his gun and use his fists. But he remained firm, determined to complete the mission.

As he was about to shoot, the Mayor shot first. Though fat and clumsy, he struck the leader and the other man, the two who were carrying machine guns.

"These guys are like little girls. If they didn't have guns, I'd make them drink out of the toilet." And he went into a disastrous boxing performance, challenging them to battle. "Get a taste of my fists, you wimps!"

The Mayor leaped around and punched the air. One of the assassins laughed at the sight. Encouraged, the Mayor continued to aim blows at the five killers. Suddenly, he turned to the side and unintentionally landed a punch on the chin of the dreamseller, who fell to the ground unconscious.

"I've killed the dreamseller!" he yelled. While trying to help him up, the Mayor couldn't bear the weight and fell on top of him, just as he'd done with Geronimo.

The hit men stifled their laughter. They saw they were dealing with bunglers, weaklings, poseurs capable of killing themselves all on their own.

"You're a disaster that walks like a man. A gutless wonder," Honeymouth told the Mayor. "You've never killed even a rat and now you want to take on these guys. This is a job for a real man." Turning toward the assassins, he said, "Use your fists first and then your bullets, you pansies."

The five men didn't hesitate. Before killing them they could vent their pent-up anger and have a little fun. They were dying to pummel these arrogant punks. And they proceeded to do so.

"Hold on! Let us get into position," said the dreamseller, trying to regain his composure.

The dreamseller and Honeymouth stood side by side. The cowardly Mayor hid behind them and, making the sign of the cross, told them, "You two start and I'll finish the job!"

It was a violent, totally uneven fight. The five criminals began beating the dreamseller and Bartholomew, first punching them and then throwing them to the ground and kicking them mercilessly.

Realizing he would die of internal bleeding, the dreamseller went back in time in his mind to see his children, and he hugged and kissed them. They seemed to be alive and implored him not to give up selling dreams, especially the dream of life. But his aggressors continued to beat him mercilessly. His fate was sealed. He was about to close the final chapter of his extraordinary history.

CHAPTER 19

At Risk of Dying

THE DREAMSELLER TRIED TO PROTECT HIMSELF, BUT IT WAS futile. His face was bleeding badly. His eyes were bruised and swollen. Sweat and blood flowing from the cut in his eyebrow blurred his vision. The trauma to his chest barely allowed him to breathe, while the blows to his skull affected his sense of balance. Bartholomew was also on the ground, bleeding from both lips. The Mayor, like a cornered animal, crouched down to protect his face, but it did no good; he was also taking a beating. They were going to die, the dreamseller thought, because of him. It was unfair.

In a fraction of a second the face of each disciple flashed through his mind. He loved them. When he seemed about to give up, the image of his children, of the wounded Bartholomew and the other disciples triggered in his brain an eruption like a volcano spewing indignation. He might die, but not without fighting for his life.

At that crucial moment, the dreamseller and Bartholomew looked at each other and gained new strength. When the attackers' leader and one of his henchmen kicked them in the stomachs, both reacted in a surprising way: they grabbed the aggressors' feet and twisted them, causing them to fall down.

The dreamseller and Bartholomew rose and assumed the

posture of martial arts experts. Although no one knew it, in reality both had been excellent fighters in the past. The dreamseller had been a black belt in karate in his youth, and Honeymouth was a specialist in jujitsu before succumbing to alcoholism.

The Mayor, though, was no fighter. His only specialty was talking. The dreamseller and Bartholomew had vowed to sell dreams in a violent society without resorting to force, but this was a special occasion. They had to choose between life and death, between the dream and the nightmare. Billions of neurons went into high gear, leading them to fight like warriors.

They pummeled the assassins masterfully, using their feet and fists. The criminals were stunned. They had never seen people so strong and determined. Now, they regretted not opening fire.

The leader aimed a kick at the neck of the Master, who skillfully deflected the blow and struck him in the chest. Gradually, the killer realized that his opponent was the better fighter. And the struggle continued. The attackers lost ground minute by minute. Two of them were almost unconscious.

In the confusion, the Mayor grabbed the guns and threw them over the wall. He never considered forcing the criminals to surrender, as he was afraid of guns and didn't even know how to pull a trigger. The leader, seeing the Mayor tossing the guns, punched him in the face, but he was quickly rescued by Honeymouth. A bit disoriented, he shouted to his friend, "Don't be a wimp, Honeymouth. Give that guy a beating he won't forget!"

The Master came to Honeymouth's aid, but a blow to the back from a henchman left him unprotected from an attack by the leader, who slammed him in the chest several times. But the dreamseller returned the blows, causing their leader to wonder,

"Where did he learn to fight like this? And how's he staying on his feet?"

The Mayor, seeing his two friends winning the battle, sat on a bench and began giving orders: "Hit him! Punch him in the face! Harder!"

A third attacker went down. Now the fight was two on two: the leader against the dreamseller, and a minion against Honeymouth. But seeing the Mayor's audacity in giving orders, the leader left the dreamseller and went after him. Running off in fright, the Mayor shouted: "Get him, Master! Get him!"

The dreamseller didn't attack him from behind. He tapped the leader on the shoulder and began displaying his full ability. He easily warded off the other's blows. And in a sudden move, hit him in the stomach and then on the right cheek. Their leader fell to the ground, and the dreamseller jumped on top of him. His eyes wide, the assassin waited for the fatal blow, but the dreamseller held up and went to help Bartholomew fight against his attacker. That was when they heard police sirens two or three blocks away.

Fearful, wounded and weakened, the attackers, as if having the victors' permission, helped one another to their feet and jumped over the high wall. They trotted away like stray dogs.

The police never arrived. They were on their way somewhere else, apparently. The three friends were left, each leaning on the other. Incredibly, Honeymouth hadn't lost his sense of humor. Just as he had done after being punched by Crusher at the independence monument, he asked, "Mayor, are we alive or in heaven?"

"I don't know about heaven, but we just left hell," he replied.

Though he was the least injured, the Mayor went limp. He was between the other two and threw his considerable weight on them to carry him.

Honeymouth asked the Master: "Boss, I never saw anybody so nimble. Where'd you learn to fight?"

"Here and there. But I'm out of shape. How about you?"

"I started in the orphanage, in classes with a Japanese man who volunteered there. Later, at a jujitsu school. But that was before I became an alcoholic and started living on the streets."

The Mayor, brazenly, didn't want to remain in the shadows. Despite being an unmitigated disaster in a fight, he still felt the need to brag. Staggering and leaning on the others, he said, "I used to teach boxing. But I'm hurt, Master."

"Why is that, Barnabas?"

"Honeymouth stood in my way and protected the bad guys. If he'd let me go, I would've made mincemeat of them." And then he winced, "Ooh, ooh! They stomped on my belly."

"You coward! If I'd let that guy get you, he would have pounded you into ground beef."

"Ha! Didn't you see what I did to their boss? I whirled in a pirouette and smacked him. I knocked him into next Tuesday," bragged the Mayor.

And they went on walking and joking, despite being beaten and injured. Since mankind first roamed the planet, pain has blocked rationality. But those two used levity to unblock it, mixing pain with laughter.

Then, in the distance, we saw three staggering men coming toward us and discovered they were the dreamseller, Bartholomew and Barnabas, leaning on one another. We couldn't believe they were alive. But at the same time, we were shaken. They were bleeding all over. Their eyes were swollen and their faces and chests were bruised, especially the dreamseller's. We needed to get them to the nearest hospital.

As soon as he saw us, the Mayor, overcome by his compulsive speech syndrome, started to brag. Although he was fatigued, his tongue was intact.

"People, I landed so many punches that the guys wet their pants." And, to demonstrate his bravery, he suddenly showed us his main blow. He raised his right fist and, not realizing that Bartholomew was beside him, hit him in the chin. Bartholomew went down in a heap. Frightened again, the Mayor said:

"Good Lord! I've killed Honeymouth!"

We had to carry him to a clearing. But we later learned the charlatan pretended to be unconscious just so we'd carry him. Such is life. Even heroes have their villainous side.

CHAPTER 20

Dangerous Association

LIVING WITH THE DREAMSELLER WAS BECOMING EXTREMELY complicated. We couldn't stop thinking about why anyone would want to kill him. Revenge? But what could he have done? To eliminate a witness? But what secrets could a man stripped of power be hiding? He denounced the madness of society but didn't name names. Was he considered a revolutionary, a threat to society? But if that were how they thought of him, why didn't they take him to court instead of eliminating him?

We had countless questions with but no answers. We didn't actually know the identity of the man we followed or what forces were conspiring against him. In the next several days, I began to become paranoid. I started shrinking from strangers, even generous people, who I thought of as potential assassins in disguise.

Bartholomew and Barnabas came to understand that following the dreamseller wasn't a bed of roses. The journey had four possible paths: praise for his brilliant ideas, ridicule and injury—or even death. Fearing for our safety, the dreamseller once again argued that it would be better for us to separate. We rejected the possibility. But how much longer and how far would we carry that torch? We didn't know.

We were not a religion, a sect or a secret society. And we

certainly didn't swear a blood oath. We were free to leave whenever we wanted. But our friendship was interwoven with a poetic kind of love. We were friends who were learning to listen to our minds, to debate the mysteries of existence and to revamp the idea of power. We were dreamers who wished to sell the dream of free emotion.

Crusher was ashamed of not having been with Bartholomew and Barnabas at the moment they most needed him. Once again the instinct for self-preservation overpowered the urge for solidarity. But they didn't hold a grudge against him. They had learned to give without expecting anything in return, a lesson I was still far from learning.

Of the three, the dreamseller was injured the worst. His right eye was bruised, and his left eyebrow and lip were split open.

Worried about blood loss, infection and possible fractures, we took him to the nearest hospital, the Mellon Lincoln Hospital. Though it was a large private facility, the most prestigious and best equipped in the city, it had a charity ward. And we were indigent.

I was uncomfortable with the hospital because it bore the name of the father of one of the nation's most important leaders, Mellon Lincoln Jr., a man I had never met personally but whose power and influence I had criticized in the classroom. He was a very wealthy businessman, and his reach extended even into my university. But his power was a thing of the past. The father, Mellon Lincoln Sr., was dead, and so was his son. Their lives were gone but their names remained.

At the entrance to the magnificent hospital, the dreamseller bumped into two men wearing impeccable suits—the director of the institution and the chief financial officer. Seeing that he had brushed against an injured beggar, the director experienced not compassion but disgust. He was starting to clean his

Valentino jacket when he noticed a bloodstain. He nervously removed the jacket and issued an abrupt order to a nearby cleaning woman, only recently hired:

"Burn it."

The woman asked, "I'm sorry, who are you?"

"What, you don't know me? I'm the director of this hospital!" he told her, dripping with arrogance.

At that moment, the director and the dreamseller made eye contact. For a few seconds the director stood there as if anesthetized. His pupils focused unblinkingly on the man he had bumped into, who was wearing an old blue jacket with three buttons missing and a bloodstained white shirt with a torn collar. The dreamseller's face seemed like a phantom to him, and not merely because of the injuries and the stained clothes he wore. Hesitantly, the director said, "Do I know you?"

"How can you know me if I don't even know myself?" the dreamseller replied.

"I once met a very important man who looked a lot like you," the director said.

"Every man is important."

The director looked the dreamseller up and down, saw his injuries, and said, "He had your courage. But fortunately, he's dead."

"There are many among the living who are also dead," the dreamseller responded.

With a haughty gaze, the director asked the dreamseller's name.

After a pause and a deep breath, the dreamseller told him, "I'm just a simple seller of dreams."

The director thought the reply bizarre. Then he saw the injured Bartholomew and the Mayor, ran his gaze over the rest of the group, and pronounced his conclusion.

"The psychiatric ward is in the rear, to the left, and the indigents' ward is to the right."

The Mayor held out his hand to thank him, not having understood the other man's arrogance. But the director turned his back, walking away without the slightest trace of sensitivity. To the man who ran the most important hospital in the city, we weren't humans but animals who needed veterinarians and a dosage of pity.

The dreamseller had always told us that most men are desperate for any type of power. The director was one of them; he had become a god. When he was ten steps ahead of us, the dreamseller called out his name: "Lucio Lobo!"

The director turned suddenly and his eyes widened as if in a horror film.

"Lucio Lobo, humility is the foundation of the wise, and pride the sin of the weak," the dreamseller told him.

The director tried to rush ahead, but as he glanced back, he bumped into a cart carrying medications and various portable medical equipment. Everything fell to the floor. The great man got up and, as if fleeing from a bomb about to go off, moved away even faster.

His CFO asked, "What's going on?"

"Nothing. Let's get out of here. I think I'm seeing things."

None of the disciples understood the significance of that moment. "How did the dreamseller know the director's name?" I wondered. "Of course," I thought. "The dreamseller is very observant and must have seen his name on his badge." But I didn't recall seeing any badge. Since he read newspapers he found in the trash, he must have read something about the director. Concerned about the dreamseller's, Bartholomew's and Barnabas's injuries, I put aside these questions and went looking for help.

After waiting in line for two hours, they were attended to without sympathy, without altruism, without kindness, like paupers who had to kneel down in gratitude for the privilege of being treated free of charge. The doctor didn't offer them a word of comfort or even ask what caused the traumas. He thought they were violent men suffering the consequences of their aggressiveness. The nurse who treated them was more generous.

After examining the dreamseller and putting in a few stitches even before the anesthesia had taken effect, the doctor took a look at Bartholomew's thorax. He seemed impatient, as if reluctantly doing us the greatest favor in the world. He made less money when he worked in the charity area than when treating private patients or those with insurance. Observing his lack of sensitivity, the dreamseller said:

"Why are you in such a rush? You're dealing with a fascinating human being."

"Right, I'm a movie star," said Honeymouth facetiously.

The doctor reacted aggressively to the dreamseller's subtle criticism. "Just who do you think you are, beggar, to address a doctor in that manner?" Then he whispered to the nurse, "I can't stand these homeless types. They've got no money but they demand everything."

"You're a doctor, you studied psychology, so why act as if you'd never heard of it?" said the dreamseller.

Loath to be confronted, the doctor again reacted, this time going further. "Look here, beggar, you people are a burden on society and on this hospital."

"Didn't the founder of this institution, Mellon Lincoln, provide conditions for doctors to treat the impoverished with the same care given to the wealthy? I guess he was wrong about a lot of things and not worthy of his power."

"What? Who are you to criticize the founder of this hospital? What gall! Just look at yourself."

After a sarcastic laugh, the doctor ended his hurried consultation and shooed them out of the examination room. He gave them a card to seek the services of a psychiatrist.

After leaving, we saw the nurse call the doctor aside and say, "Doctor, that's the man who's been stirring up the city."

"That's him? I can't believe it! We were talking about him just the other day. Why didn't you say anything?"

He felt he had missed a chance to explore the mind of a genius. Yes, he had let slip through his fingers the opportunity to buy some dreams. Instead, he would go on wallowing in his tiny world.

CHAPTER 21

Ten Minutes to Silence a Life

WE WERE CROSSING THE MAIN LOBBY OF THE HOSPITAL ON our way out. Suddenly, two men in white, with stethoscopes dangling from their necks, spoke to us very graciously, asking if we had been treated well and apologizing for any misunderstanding. They looked at the dreamseller and, without asking permission, began examining his lumbar region and listening to the left side of his chest. They decided he needed additional treatment. They examined Bartholomew and the Mayor as well but told them they were fine.

They insisted we go with them. The dreamseller wanted to leave, but Monica and Jurema asked them to complete the examination. He was determined to leave. Then the group glutton intervened. "I'm feeling weak," the Mayor said. "If I don't get something to eat I'm gonna faint." And he began exhibiting what he assumed were signs of dizziness.

"Of course, sir. We've prepared a meal for you and anyone else who cares to come," they said.

"You need to mind your health," said the Mayor as he and Bartholomew each took one of the dreamseller's arms and pushed him toward the new examination room and, obviously, toward their next meal.

Crusher and Edson joined them in the other room to eat. Jurema and Monica stayed with me. After examining him, they said the dreamseller needed medicine and asked me to wait outside, but I refused. Monica and Jurema sat outside. They located a vein and hooked up the IV, injecting some ten vials of what they said was glucose and antibiotics. They said the dreamseller would fall asleep briefly and that they would return in ten minutes.

I was suspicious and rummaged through the trash to see what they had added to the serum. It was fentanyl, an anesthetic. "Anesthetic?" I thought. Despite not being a doctor, I knew that in a few minutes he would be dead. The dreamseller had also pinched shut the IV feed as soon as they left. He, too, was suspicious.

We immediately removed the needle from his arm. I called in Jurema and Monica to help me and we rushed out of there. I asked them to call Bartholomew, Barnabas and the others, and we quickly left the hospital.

Once we were outside, the dreamseller looked sadly at the walls and the equally cold people who worked inside them. He knew that inside those walls, money had become more important than life.

We went to our old home, Kennedy Bridge. Professor Jurema wanted us to go to her mansion, but the dreamseller declined because there were more risks to come, and he didn't want to involve her or us. He asked Bartholomew and Barnabas to go with her, but they refused to leave his side.

Jurema and Monica bought ice packs and medicine and looked after him until nightfall. And before saying good-bye to the women and Crusher, the dreamseller asked us to gather in a circle.

"All of you have been a source of happiness. You've taught me, each in your own way, that it is worthwhile to invest in humanity. But it's time we parted ways."

"What are you saying?" asked Jurema. "We're a family!"

"My dear Jurema, we can no longer travel together. You're all too important to me to be put at risk. I don't know how much longer I have to live. Please, don't insist. Each of us must follow his own path."

"But, Master," said Monica, with tears in her eyes, "if we're in danger here, we can go to another city, another state, even another country."

"My enemies are powerful. They will pursue me to the ends of the earth."

When I heard that, I couldn't bear it anymore.

"Master, I know that you have never made us talk about our past unless it was of our own free will. So please forgive me for invading your privacy. Who are those enemies and why do they want to kill you?"

He looked into my eyes and apologized for not wishing to go into details about his background. "Whoever knows my secrets is at risk. Because of my love for all of you, there are certain secrets I cannot reveal."

He paused and showed us his chest and back, both of which bore large scars. And he told us as much as it was possible to tell:

"These scars are from a fire, the first time they tried to kill me. And they almost succeeded. A charred body was found, that of a good man without a family, who lived in the streets as we do. I hired him to be my gardener and had long conversations with him, came to know his traumas and his pain. I gave him a gift, a ring with an image of two children that symbolized my son and daughter, as thanks for listening to me and serving me. One day we were talking and there was an explosion. Flames spread rapidly through the house. My friend died, and they thought it was me. My enemies were quiet until they discovered I was still alive."

"But why do they want to kill you?" insisted Dimas.

He hesitated before replying. He wanted us to love him for what he was and not for what he possessed. He wanted us to sell dreams because it was the greatest project for a human being and not because of the influence of some powerful figure. All he said was this:

"Money attracts enemies and drives away friends. I have nothing, yet you insist on staying. I'm close to death, but you don't abandon me. You are truly my friends."

"If we're your friends, don't ask us to leave," said the Mayor, his voice choked with emotion.

The next day, the front page of the city's major newspapers carried headlines saying that the gentle, calm man who claimed to sell dreams and denounced violence had shown an aggressive side. Ignorant of the facts, they distorted the dreamseller's image, but because he was no slave to public opinion, he continued on his journey.

We said good-bye to Jurema, Monica and Crusher, and lay down to sleep. The night was touch and go. Sleep barely came. I can't say if the cold rattling my bones was caused by the weather or the anxiety reverberating in my body.

We woke up several times, frightened. Honeymouth was also experiencing an agitated sleep; three times he punched the air, feeling pains in his body. The Mayor woke up in the middle of the night and slipped away unnoticed. He came back at two in the morning with a few shots of vodka in him. It was his first relapse since joining the dreamseller.

The Master asked our patience as the Mayor tried to give another speech:

"On this glorious night, I would like to promise you that I'll send you to hell if you don't vote for me," he mumbled. But he was tired and quickly fell back to sleep. In half an hour he was snoring like a horse.

Finally, the sun woke us up to the sound of sparrows, pigeons and other birds, singing despite the storm the previous night. I thought to myself that we're the only species that thinks and that thinking is both a privilege and a curse.

Sitting on his worn mattress pad and inspired by the birdsong and the sunlight filtering through the bridge, the dreamseller, though injured and marked for death, began to sing:

I thought I couldn't lose.
But in the very core of my being,
My heroism crumbled,
My confidence was shattered.
And now that I've discovered myself,
I will not despair.
Until death finds me,
Like a bird I would take
From each day its greatest melody.

Dimas took out his harmonica and started playing along. We celebrated life in the early hours of dawn. We knew we were going to die, but in an all-too-brief existence we wanted to take from each day its greatest melody. Fear could not spoil our celebration.

We got up famished and quickly found Monica, Jurema and the other followers. We taught them our new song. It was seven o'clock on a sunny Saturday, and the sunrise was enchanting.

An hour later, we stopped by the bakery owned by Gutemberg, a seventy-year-old Portuguese man who was afraid people would eat and not pay their bill.

"Gutemberg, my good man," said Honeymouth, trying to butter up the baker, "you have the privilege of serving this notable group of hungry people."

"Man of bread and dough, when I assume the leadership of this nation, you will be my head chef," added the Mayor.

The baker twisted his mustache with his left hand and rubbed his right index finger and thumb together, indicating that he wanted money. The Mayor tried another tack.

"Then you can be my minister of industry!" Gutemberg continued to make the money-sign. "How about economics minister?" But still no bread was forthcoming. Then he appealed. "Invest in this man of the future!" he said, tapping his chest like the craziest politician I'd ever seen.

We got up a collection to buy our breakfast. Jurema and the other women who followed the dreamseller often supplied some of our necessities when they were present, but he discouraged them from bringing more money than they would need in a day.

But Jurema, who was in the beginning stages of Alzheimer's, forgot her purse at home. She didn't even have money for her own meal.

Gutemberg, though outwardly gruff, had saved us a dozen times with stale bread that he wouldn't be able to sell the next day. Milk, coffee and bread and butter brought joy to our taste buds, especially because we didn't always eat dinner, or at least not in an adequate fashion.

The night before, we ate the remains of spaghetti that a nearby Italian restaurant was about to throw out. Edson, the Miracle Worker, begged the cook and managed a small, cold plate of spaghetti that was scarcely enough to quiet their hunger pangs. Restaurants seldom gave leftovers to the homeless for fear of making them sick and becoming the target of lawsuits. One more way the system punished the poor.

CHAPTER 22

A Human Being's Worst Enemies

OUR BRIEF CAMARADERIE AT GUTEMBERG'S BAKERY allowed us to forget the recent dangers we had survived. Once again the Portuguese baker's stale bread saved the Mayor, though it took three helpings to line his stomach.

The dreamseller appeared concentrated but calm. He left after having breakfast. As always, he went off without telling us where he was headed. We quickly followed him, and after about twenty minutes arrived at a beautiful garden.

Multicolored butterflies floated everywhere, and humming-birds hovered in the air, contemplating hibiscus flowers before extracting their nectar. At my university there was also an immense oval garden, but I had never spent any time learning its secrets. I thought life only pulsed in the classroom or in the professors' lounge.

Where there is only knowledge, anguish flourishes. Joyless thoughts are like an existence without flowers. In my department we overvalued reason and crushed emotion. We were unbalanced and specialists in conflict. It was a rare intellectual who hadn't made enemies.

The dreamseller taught me simple but fundamental things. To him, reason and emotion were never separate. He trained us in the art of internalizing, observing, reasoning through deduction and induction. He taught us to lose ourselves in the details before looking at the big picture. Our eyes were like a film director's, capturing tiny details imperceptible to someone who was inattentive. We experienced grand emotions over small events. We were envied even by celebrities who met us.

In a time when suicide rates were climbing a hundred percent each decade, especially in affluent nations, we were obsessed with life.

As soon as we entered the garden, a Muslim leader with a few of his followers approached the dreamseller and kissed him, eager to hear what he had to say. Just ahead, an Orthodox Jew, accompanied by several boys, did the same. They all wanted to listen to him. A group of twenty women from another institution were there to drink in droplets of his wisdom. And I asked myself, "What kind of man is this who attracts such different people?"

During the walk, the dreamseller asked us to observe the trees and imagine ourselves to be the dry leaves falling from the small branches, floating carefree until reaching the ground, where we would enrich the soil with their our bodies.

"In the end, a person's purpose is to enrich the society in which he lives. Living only for ourselves negates our existential role," he said.

Everything seemed perfect that morning. But traveling with the dreamseller was unpredictable. He slowed his pace and stood before the group, looking down in concentration. Everyone stopped and tried to see what he was seeing. Actually, he was absorbed in observing the small weeds growing in the cracked concrete. He was dazzled by the miniature round leaves that formed dark-green bouquets.

How can a wise man spend time on weeds that not even the most dedicated gardener would notice? It seemed like a waste of his intelligence. But he didn't care about public opinion or ours. He bent down and muttered a few almost inaudible words. But we read his lips.

"Heroic weeds. You are born in inhospitable places, without water and almost without soil, and you resist the indifference of passersby. You are like street children who stubbornly cling to life. I salute you."

What he said was passed from mouth to mouth, for all to hear. Seeing us watching him, he stood up and, without explanation, said:

"If the world were at war with you, the battle might be bearable, but if you're at war with yourself, it is unbearable. Without facing your internal enemies, it's almost impossible not to create mental wars—or to survive them."

"What war is he talking about?" I thought. While I was pondering the matter, Bartholomew, who specialized in reacting without thinking, said, "Boss, I'm a man of peace. I don't have any enemies."

"I wish that were so, Bartholomew, but we humans are experts in creating them, even the wisest among us. And the worst enemies are those we don't see or can't admit."

The Mayor insisted he, too, was a man without enemies. He had forgotten that the night before he had done battle with his own imagination.

"Dreamseller, I'm a conci—conci—" He stumbled over the words. Then, furious at himself, said, "Out, you blasted word!" Trying again, he succeeded: "I'm a conciliator of ideas. The problems I have come from conspiracy by the opposition." And he looked at me as if I were part of the group that opposed him.

The dreamseller must have thought, "What am I doing here with this band of incorrigibles?" But he said patiently:

"I'm speaking of a war fought by great and small, by rich and poor. A war that takes the shine from celebrities, sleep from the religious, serenity from intellectuals, and transforms the courageous into cowards. I'm speaking of a war that we have imported from society around us."

He continued. "I'm talking about the war concealed behind smiles, disguised by the culture, covered up by philanthropic gestures, hidden by the tyranny of fashion and dark glasses."

The dreamseller then spoke with an astuteness unlike any I had ever heard, about the setbacks suffered since man first acted out his existential play on the enigmatic stage of time.

"Some entrench themselves against their fears, others against an excess of euphoria. Some do battle with their worries, others with their alienation. Some are haunted by fixed ideas, others by morbid thoughts. Some are frightened of the future, others of the past. Some struggle against excessive saving, others against compulsive spending. Who is brought up to survive in this war? Who is trained to escape unharmed or with minimal trauma?"

No one, I thought. I had never seen the slightest mention of this subtle war within the human mind or how to equip oneself to survive it. Hundreds of billions of dollars were spent to train and equip soldiers for wars that drain blood, but no one was training us to combat what drains us of altruism, creativity and wisdom.

I knew that over seventy percent of students suffered from anxiety. The epidemic of anxiety was denied by academics. More and more I agreed with the dreamseller that the educational system was sick, producing sick people for a sick society.

I was sick. I had to admit I was tormented by worries, unresolved conflict, feelings of guilt and jealousy, a neurotic need to control others and many other demons. While I thought about my war, the dreamseller spoke of his:

"Today I'm a person in rags, but I was once a man envied and considered invincible. Everyone was familiar with my outward armor, but they didn't know I was unprotected in the one place where I should have been most secure. I was beaten, defeated. But, when everyone thought I would never recover from my irreparable losses, I reunited with myself. I rose from the ashes. I haven't destroyed the ghosts in my mind; my mission is to tame them, discipline them."

Many tried to hide their mistakes, but the dreamseller exuded sincerity in facing them. He didn't promote himself, didn't speak about his wealth, his academic background, his social status. He spoke only about what was essential. Then the philosophical prophet shocked us with these words:

"I have always told you that the weak attack, but the strong are tolerant. Now I ask you not to be tolerant with your ghosts. Fight with all your strength against everything that disturbs your mind. Either conquer your worries or they will conquer you. Tame your feelings of guilt or they will make you their slave. Shout, go into a rage against negative states of mind, fixed ideas, alienation, compulsion. There are no giants. Share your battles with your friends. And if you don't win, look for professional help. Existence is too precious to be confined in a cell."

It was the first time he told us to rage, not against others but against our phantoms. It was the first time he recommended we seek out a psychiatrist or psychologist if necessary. I thought he detested them. We plunged into a state of silence, broken suddenly by our resident psychologist:

"People, I've got experience! And I'm charging just fifty bucks a consult," said Bartholomew, evoking laughter from those present. Yes, he had "experience" all right—in complicating other people's problems.

"That man has already driven five psychologists nuts!" said Edson of Bartholomew. The Miracle Worker had always been religious but never recognized his fallacies.

"Slander! I'm a complex man in search of simplification,"

said Bartholomew effusively. "Whoever doesn't simplify me complicates me. I'm a genius!"

The Mayor, hearing this, felt obligated to outdo him. "Folks, although I'm more intelligent than this bigmouth, I charge only a sandwich for therapy."

"But, Mayor, you've already given three psychiatrists heart attacks," said Monica, needling him.

"Yes, but, but—" The Mayor couldn't think of anything to refute Monica. He called on Bartholomew for help. "I'll let my secretary of education answer."

"The Mayor gave psychiatrists heart attacks because his illness is inexplicable and untreatable."

Believing he had been praised, he kissed Bartholomew on his swollen eye. I never knew if the Mayor was naïve or the shrewdest of us all. Excited, he thanked Bartholomew for his words: "Great men need to be followed by stagnant minds."

"Stagnant?" said Honeymouth, neither understanding nor liking the term. But the group's politician explained without explaining:

"Stagnant with information. Having a brain impregnated and bewildered with old data." But now Bartholomew understood even less than before. He didn't know whether he was being insulted or commended.

I started thinking it was time for academic curriculums to undergo major surgery, and perhaps the dreamseller might one day be among the surgeons. Our students destroyed themselves, becoming sick, depressed, and we simply denied the psychic phenomena that assailed them. Whenever one of them committed suicide, we were stunned, secretly nursing our feelings of guilt.

We took refuge behind textbooks and exams, as if exams measured a true education. Often, exams were a cloak to hide the madness of an educational system and disguise our alienation.

CHAPTER 23

Women with Complex Minds

THE DREAMSELLER NEVER CHASTISED US. EVEN KNOWING
we could be ridiculous sometimes, he encouraged us to
debate. Simply walking among this group turned your world
into a circus.

That's why, more and more, it wasn't just intellectuals who
followed us but also groups of young people. We discovered
that this was because certain psychiatrists and psychologists
were advising some of their patients suffering from anxiety and
depression to seek out others like them. It seemed that this unusual group had a potentiating effect on antidepressants and
tranquilizers.

I suspected the dreamseller had chosen our group of misfits to help temper his ideas. He was serious and focused, but
through us, he taught playfully. The problem was that my
friends got carried away, putting him and other disciples in
precarious situations.

I used to teach both students and university faculty. I never
kidded around in the classroom, never used humor in my lessons. My classes were a restaurant where people ate out of
obligation. And to think I was considered the most eloquent
member of the faculty.

The dreamseller never set the locations of his open-air classroom, nor the hour when he was going to speak, much less the subject he would discuss. Nevertheless, people of all ages, cultures, and levels of education sought him out, eager to hear him. In contrast, I used to set a time, place and topic but people weren't excited to hear me. It's sad to say, but were it not for the tests, my classroom would have been empty.

While I was thinking about my past, the politician decided it was time to speak. The Mayor, elated at the number of women in the audience, which included a mix of Jews, Muslims, young people and other potential followers, started into his speech:

"Beloved voters of this generous city. As one of the leaders with the broadest vision of the future among this mass of mortals, I would like to tell you that women are more intelligent, gracious, sensible, wise and creative than men."

The dreamseller applauded. Monica, Professor Jurema and the other women also applauded enthusiastically. I thought to myself, "Here he goes again, trying to upstage the dreamseller." But to keep up appearances, I applauded as well.

Seeing the women applauding vigorously, he bellowed, "Buuut . . ."

Several of the women rolled their eyes, figuring the Mayor never dished out praise without strings attached.

Then he added playfully, "But they invented shopping centers!"

The women burst into laughter, and all the men, including me, joined them. They admitted that the compulsion to buy was one of their worst enemies. I couldn't understand how the guy managed to be so funny. Encouraged by his "truthful joke," I decided to risk being playful.

"From their hair to their toenails, women have something to spend money on. How did you manage that feat?" I asked.

Dimas, a con man who had stolen women's purses in the past, chimed in with this joke, stuttering only slightly:

"People, these days you d—don't need ultrasound to know the child's sex. You just run a credit card over the woman's belly. If it's a girl, the child starts kicking like crazy."

Everyone laughed and felt at ease. As always, Bartholomew couldn't keep his mouth shut. But he seemed quiet as if meditating. It was the first time he wasn't flamboyant.

"Are you sick, Bartholomew? Do you have a headache?" Monica asked.

Monica was naïve. Encouraged, he could cause the biggest headache of the morning. And he did. Clearing his throat, he said, "Beautiful Monica, most intelligent Jurema and all the other women hearing me. You are more magnanimous than men!"

"Magnanimous?" I thought. I wonder if he even knows the meaning of that word. As if reading my mind he continued:

"For those who don't know, 'magnanimous' means giving, benevolent, generous, charitable."

The women applauded. Seduced by this lunatic, they hung on every word. And he went on. "If not for a woman, my brain and I wouldn't be here." We laughed at that piece of foolishness.

"What about your father? Didn't he participate in your construction? Or were you by some chance cloned?" asked a Muslim man.

"Yes, Daddy spent nine minutes and Mom spent nine months in that construction. It's with good reason that Jews consider that only someone with a Jewish mother is genuinely Jewish." And imitating the dreamseller, he said, "I bow before you women!"

An Orthodox Jew applauded him spiritedly. And the women were won over, too. Extremely excited, Honeymouth continued his exaltation of women:

"Wandering through the labyrinths of my privileged mind,

I recall a story that demonstrates the superiority of women. I was once walking along a beautiful beach in Miami, thinking about the mysteries of life, when suddenly a dazzling bottle washed ashore from the far corners of the Atlantic. Like any curious person, I opened it. And do you know what was in it?" he asked the audience.

"Money!" the Mayor guessed.

"No, my friend. A genie! But a stressed, agitated, irritated genie like my friend the Mayor. The genie was so impatient that he hurriedly told me, 'You get three wishes, but I can only grant one. Hurry up, I have a therapy session I need to get to!' The genie's world had also turned into a giant mental institution, like ours. And this genie was brilliant and insane, like our Julio Cesar. I told him emphatically, 'I want to visit Cuba!'

"'Cuba? Is that all?' the genie asked, happy to get rid of me so easily.

"'Yes, I want to visit Cuba, *but* . . . I'm afraid of planes and boats. So I want you to build a bridge from Miami to Cuba!'

"'What? A bridge that long? Are you crazy?' And he grumbled, 'Gimme a break. Do you have any idea the amount of planning and engineering that goes into building a bridge? Much less one that long? Forget it, wish for something else.'

"So he asked me for my second wish, adding, 'Remember, money is tight, so I can only grant one wish.'"

Bartholomew paused before continuing with the craziest story ever.

"So then I asked him about the desire of every politician, executive and economist. I told him: 'I want to know how the world economy works, the logic behind it, and how to prevent new crises.' When he heard my second wish, the genie started panting and having stomach cramps. He grabbed his stomach and said, 'Tell me your third wish. And make it fast.'"

Bartholomew paused again. No one blinked.

"Then, people, in a stroke of extreme lucidity, I announced my third and final extraordinary wish. A wish that thinkers and philosophers of every era have dreamed of."

"Out with it!" we yelled, bursting with curiosity.

"That's what the genie said: 'Out with it! Out with it!' I looked him in the eye and said, 'Genie, my wish is simple. I want to understand the mind of women!'" When he heard my third wish, he groaned and asked almost breathlessly, 'So, do you want that bridge to Cuba to be two lanes or four?'"

People were falling over with laughter. The women in the crowd also laughed uncontrollably. But good-naturedly, they went after Bartholomew.

Professor Jurema hooked her cane around his neck. Surrounded by the women, she said, "Women really are complex. So complex that we were kept quiet for centuries for fear of our intelligence."

Once things calmed down, the dreamseller spoke.

"It's obvious that the socioeconomic system over the ages has been male-dominated and riddled with errors," he said. "Men's reckless ambition has generated wars, religious conflicts, discrimination, financial crises, predatory competition in international commerce. I would like to see women become heads of state across the world. If they act like their male counterparts, they will commit the same mistakes. But if they act along the lines of their intuition, femininity, generosity and sensitivity they will change history."

I remembered reading sociological texts about the behaviors of men and women. Men always committed more crimes, more acts of exclusion and were more violent and corrupt than women. Their instincts were different.

And just like that, just as the wind blows unexpectedly and without course, the dreamseller went on his way. Wandering was his fate, thinking was his commitment.

CHAPTER 24

The Greatest Inventory

VARIOUS INTERESTING EVENTS HAPPENED THAT WEEK. I took countless notes on scrap paper. One day I must compile them. Since I'm relating selected events, admitting that my criteria are fallible and distorted, I want to tell you about an incident that occurred the following Saturday, one that penetrated the depths of my mind. Something I never imagined could happen.

Our group was passing by the building that housed the city's most important civil registry. There was an enormous public square nearby, an isolated spot rarely bustling with people. But now, counting the closest disciples and casual followers, there were close to forty of us. In our group were five psychology students and six medical students in their last year of school. All of them had taken part in other meetings, so they were familiar with us.

As soon as we arrived, we saw two identical twins walking by us arguing about the inheritance they were to receive. Each of them had a lawyer at his side. They had spent hours trying in vain to reach an agreement about the estate. The twins had been the best of friends before the death of their father, apparently inseparable, but they became enemies after the reading of the will. One of them wanted to sue the other.

The dreamseller looked at them and suddenly asked us about the most important possessions of a human being. "Who among you has made an inventory of the most significant facts that constitute the quilt of your story?"

"Inventory? What do you mean?" Monica asked.

The dreamseller replied, "Making an inventory of our story is much more than just thinking about the past. Making an inventory is to describe the most relevant facts of one's own self. It's bringing together the pieces and reorganizing them. It's being an engineer of the mind who builds bridges between his experiences."

And, gazing at the students in the audience, he said, "We're a fragmented society made up of fragmented people. What is the relationship between losses and pleasure, between despair and peace? What is the bridge between fear and tranquillity? Are they irreconcilable? Is depression completely separate from joy, or can it provide us with a map for finding it?"

The psychology students looked at one another blankly. They had never studied anything about bridges between fear and tranquillity, between depression and joy. They were familiar with theories and diagnoses of mental disturbances but hadn't discussed the construct of a mental map capable of connecting different experiences to promote learning and maturity. The medical students were equally puzzled.

"Many thinkers have died without building bridges between the power of analysis and the power of happiness, between painstaking observation and the contemplation of existence, between internalization and socialization," the dreamseller said.

He managed to blend psychology, sociology, philosophy and pedagogy. Great men were fractured individuals. Newton was antisocial. Einstein had depressive traits. They were experts in some areas but fragile in others. Perhaps they never thought of building bridges between the elements of their past.

"Where are the celebrities who have managed to reconcile their inventory and established connections between social success and emotional success? And the great journalists? Who among them learned to erect bridges between criticism and relaxation? The great politicians of history—who among them built byways throughout their lives capable of connecting power and simplicity, between being constantly in the spotlight and an awareness of their vulnerability? Whoever doesn't construct mental bridges builds instead islands in the cerebral cortex. One moment he may be a lamb, the next moment a lion. At one moment calm, explosive at another. In these times of collective anxiety, youth the world over experience that drama," he said.

I sat down to reflect on this information. I didn't know if it was correct, but for the first time I heard coherent explanations for the contradictions in human behavior. I had never understood why the reactions of the great men of history fluctuated between extremes. Their cerebral cortexes weren't continents, rather, they were made up of islands.

"Caligula was insignificant but thought he was more beautiful than Rome," the Master continued. "He had outbursts of kindness and fits of fury. Nero was a young man given to the arts but became one of the most brutal men in history, never thinking twice about killing those who opposed him. Stalin ordered the murder of supposed enemies at night and the next morning had breakfast with their wives as if nothing had happened. Hitler patted and fed his dog, but starved and froze to death a million Jewish children."

The dreamseller paused to let us reflect critically on his ideas. But there wasn't time; the Mayor shattered the silence.

"My people, I'm a man of bridges," he said with a politician's pride. "If I come to power, I'll build bridges throughout the city. I'll be quicker than Honeymouth's genie. I'll build bridges between city hall and the shantytowns. I'll build bridges between Congress and the city's psych wards."

Encouraging his friend, Honeymouth said, "Very good, noble Mayor. I request you build bridges between the banks and the cemeteries."

"Why, Bartholomew?" asked Solomon.

"Because that's where my friends in debt are." And he took out a handkerchief to dry his crocodile tears.

"Wait, didn't you say they're buried in the banks themselves?" Crusher said, cutting in.

"Yes, but there's not enough room for so many bankrupt people."

This time they buried the dreamseller's ideas, mixing fractured minds with bankrupt people, politicians with insane asylums. A real jumble. But the dreamseller was happy to see his disciples reflect on these questions.

"When someone dies, an inventory is made of his goods. But which are the most relevant—jewels, cars, houses, stocks, farmland?" he asked. "None of these! It's the body of experiences that make us historical beings. A human being without history is a book without letters. We must make an inventory of the most frustrating and the most joyful experiences of our lives and give it out to those we love, while we're still alive."

And then he looked up at the tall buildings and began shouting like a madman.

"No pain should be borne without bridges of relief being built. No shortcoming should be corrected without a lesson learned. Otherwise, suffering is useless. There is no truth to the idea that pain serves to enrich character. Unless we make certain connections, pain worsens the human being, fear traumatizes him, guilt smothers him," he said.

These last words made me recall my several therapy sessions. My therapists urged me to stir up the innards of my past, agonize over my conflicts, but I couldn't recall them. I felt powerless.

I would walk the streets panting, gasping for air, my muscles aching, my memory failing, unable to remember everyday facts. My mental energy was exhausted. I felt like a hundred-year-old man in the body of someone in his forties.

When I was in crisis, I had no bridges to my successes. My crises lasted forever. When I was in anguish, I had no channels to wake me and make me see that my life wasn't a loss, that it was in fact bright with color and joy. The windows of my brain could shine into one another. I carried around a library in my head, but I was an isolated intellectual, lonely and miserable.

CHAPTER 25

The Inventory of Five Traumas and Their Bridges

O VERHEARING THE DREAMSELLER'S LECTURE TO THE psychology and medical students was Fernando Lataro, warden of the famous maximum security prison nicknamed "Demons Island." He was accompanied by two police officers and three educators from the prison. He was a weekend follower, as it was difficult for him to leave work, the comforts of home and his cars to become a wanderer with no place to live or anything to eat.

"Whoever doesn't learn to mine the gold in his own life will never be able to improve himself and overcome," the dreamseller had said.

Some of my students were cocaine or marijuana addicts, others were addicted to gambling and still others were compulsive spenders. When it came to relationships, some had fits of jealousy and became paranoid when rejected, while others changed partners the way you change clothes. Some lived in fear of not succeeding in life, while others were alienated as if there were no tomorrow. Neither of us had learned to sort out our history and bring together our extremes.

The dreamseller asked his listeners to sift through their past and reflect on the five most anguished moments of their lives, in descending order of suffering, from greatest to least. He also asked us to analyze the bridges we had built or should have built between these and other episodes of our story.

We remained silent for an hour, prospecting for anguishing facts that had marked us. Some sat on benches, others on the ground, and some remained standing. It was a fascinating experience.

After the exercise came the big revelation. The dreamseller had us sit in a circle and said that whoever felt free to do so could describe those five episodes and comment on one of them. He emphasized, "Don't talk unless you feel comfortable."

I thought no one was going to open up. We were all inhibited at first. After two long minutes, incredibly, Edson spoke up, and what he said surprised us. The man who loved to perform miracles for self-promotion had descended to the lowest level of the human condition. He took an inventory of his anguish, a declaration he had never made to anyone except his God.

He spoke of the five most painful episodes in his life starting with the most troubling. I never imagined anyone could dissect his soul so transparently.

"One: I was sexually abused as a child. Two: I lost my mother when I was a teenager. Three: I was publicly humiliated at work. Four: My father beat me when I was thirteen. Five: I lost my best friend to cancer when I was fifteen."

That scale of suffering demonstrated that the sexual abuse was more agonizing than the loss of his mother. While the loss of his mother was indescribable, the pain of sexual abuse was almost irreparable, at least for Edson. The sequence also showed that, to him, being humiliated publicly was more painful than losing his best friend to cancer. The public humiliation caused a rupture in his personality. That might explain why he was always trying to promote himself.

"I learned that to violate the intimacy of a child is a crime that destroys the springtime of our history. I learned that behind the least suspicious people and the most innocent conversations can hide inhuman psychopaths who don't think about the consequences of their actions and want only to satisfy their instincts."

Edson said that before the abuse, he was extroverted, free and outgoing, but after those episodes—there was more than one—he lost his spontaneity, his sociability, and withdrew into himself. He became dispirited, turned inward excessively. He grew up feeling rage for the parents who hadn't protected him, and hatred toward his aggressor. He dreamed every day of strangling him or throwing him off a cliff. And, he said, in his relationship with God he had found mechanisms of tolerance and a brake to soften his instincts.

"But unfortunately I didn't build a bridge of dialogue. At first I kept quiet because of the psychopath's blackmail. Later I kept quiet out of shame. Finally, I kept quiet because I thought I had overcome my conflict, but I was in denial that some of its roots were still active in my personality."

He said that since joining the dreamseller he had begun to see there are other ways of violating someone's trust, such as blackmailing him or pressuring him to accept your ideas and truths.

Some intellectuals commit that kind of abuse, I reflected. They violate the mind of those who disagree with them and who depend on them. I'm a socialist intellectual and supposedly a humanist, but I now see there's an animal in my intellect eager to devour whatever defenseless minds dare to contradict me.

Edson concluded his remarkable exposition by saying, "I hope to grow to understand the difference between exposing and imposing our thoughts."

It's a pity I had never asked my students to make an inventory of their histories. Of course, they wouldn't need to recount them in public, but today I think that if they had learned even the fundamentals of being prospectors of their minds, they'd run less risk of being slaves to their conflicts.

Edson's story moved me. I had considered him a charlatan, an egomaniac, a religious wastrel. But at that moment, I was ashamed of my shallowness. I didn't know him, even though we had spent months sleeping next to one another. Now I understand that behind his anxious drive to make his presence known is the vital need to be accepted. Am I any better than he? Not at all. My authoritarianism in the classroom stemmed from a sick need to be socially accepted. Behind every authoritarian is a child wanting to be loved.

We applauded Edson for having the courage to dissect his history and for the bridges he had built.

Monica gave him a long hug. "You're incredible! I believe in miracles. Especially the miracle of friendship. Anyone who has friends has a treasure," she told him.

The Mayor and Honeymouth lifted him onto their shoulders, singing and playfully joking with him. And they took advantage of the situation to tweak me: "For Edson's a jolly good fellow! For Edson's a jolly good fellow! Not annoying like Julio Cesaaaar! Which nobody can deny."

CHAPTER 26

Dammed-up Pain

S OLOMON WAS THE SECOND TO TELL US HIS INVENTORY. Though he had suffered some relapses, his tics and his hypochondria had lessened as he walked with the dreamseller. But as he began talking about himself, his compulsive behavior worsened. He began opening and closing his mouth repeatedly and putting his hand on his chest to see if his heart was still beating. He made the inventory of his five greatest dramas as follows.

"First, I was humiliated at school. Second, I lost my parents in an accident. Third, I went hungry as an adolescent. Fourth, I suffered burns as a child. Fifth, I was in a car accident."

I was surprised by the scale of his issues. I realized I understood very little about psycho-sociological matters. Solomon loved his parents. They were generous and sociable. Their loss when he was fourteen struck at the roots of his being, shook his structure, but, as incredible as it seems, that wasn't the worst crisis of his life—being publicly humiliated at school was his worst existential experience. Which indicates that there are episodes that go unnoticed by psychiatrists and psychologists but are more relevant than our science can imagine.

To clear away any doubts, Solomon described the apex of his drama:

"My obsessions always attracted the attention of my class-mates. And even as I would overcome one mania, another would appear. I used to jump up and down five times before entering the classroom so no one would die; I would slap my forehead; I would feel my neck constantly looking for signs of cancer; I coughed all the time; I would repeat the last five words someone said on the phone; count the windows in a building I passed; look for holes to stick my finger in."

We were all astonished at how the young man had suffered. After a pause to collect his thoughts, he continued.

"One day when I was thirteen my classmates held a surprise party for me," he said. "I was happy as could be. They brought out a cake, and the boys and girls started singing 'Happy Birth-day.' Then I saw the words they had written on the cake: Psycho Solomon. I ran away, crying. To this day, birthday parties make my skin crawl."

And he added that several times during recess, when his incessant hand gestures were out of control, students from all the other grades would form a circle around him and start to scream, "Crazy!" and hit him on the head. The principal, seeing Solomon's tics, tried to hide a smile. He never reprimanded the other students or helped to build any bridges between those whose behavior was different.

"Going to school became a torment. It was like being in the Coliseum in front of a bloodthirsty mob. I wanted to die, to disappear from the world. When my parents died, I went hungry for a year, but nothing was as severe as the hunger for understanding. I didn't want the other students to love me, but for them to treat me like a person and not like a circus animal."

After a brief pause considering this difficult chapter of his life, he continued.

"The years passed and I built bridges," he said. "A psychia-trist helped me. With her I learned that, despite being obsessive I wasn't a piece of trash, I was a human being. But I didn't learn certain fundamental bridges. I should have learned what the dreamseller has taught us, to not demand from others what they can't give, because those closest to us are the ones who cause us disappointment. How could I demand understanding from my colleagues if they were at war with themselves?"

Solomon took a breath, deeply relieved. He had lost the fear of being who he was. He slept under bridges but had learned to feel like a human being, a star in the theater of society. By making his inventory he let cool air into some of the suffocating corners of his mind. I stood up and embraced him as if he were my son.

"You're one of the anonymous heroes Hollywood never makes movies about," I told him. "A social actor more brilliant than the brightest stars. Congratulations!"

Bartholomew got up and also hugged Solomon. "Dude, you're beautiful! I'm obsessively crazy about you."

The Mayor, more unrestrained, said, "I'm going to cover you with kisses." And he moved toward him. But Solomon ducked his head and ran as we all laughed.

After applauding him, Professor Jurema also gave her powerful inventory. I never could have imagined that behind that remarkable woman, admired by the leading educational figures in the country, lay a tormented soul. I never guessed from reading her books and articles that behind them was a terribly wounded child. I have to revise my process of interpretation, build bridges in my mind to read between the lines.

"The mental illness of my father was the saddest chapter in my life. After that was the passing of my beloved twin brother when I was ten years old. My third dilemma came when I had breast cancer. Next was the loss of my husband. And the fifth was the battles I had against the educational system."

The loss of her brother, breast cancer, the loss of her beloved husband all shook her world, but nothing rocked that solid professor as much as her father's mental illness at a time when treatment was inadequate and prejudice was rife.

"My father," she said, taking a deep breath, "was my hero, my friend, my support, my safe harbor. He was the person who loved me most in this life and the one I loved most. He owned a large grocery store. He was a brilliant and humane businessman. He was the oldest child and helped raise his six siblings. He was so humane that he gave what he had to whomever needed it, without receiving anything in return. My mother detested that in him. My father couldn't see anyone going hungry without coming to their aid. Whenever he put together a food basket for a needy family, he would take me with him. To him, giving wasn't a burden but a celebration. Investing in human beings was his joy."

"Walking with the Master," she said, turning to the dreamseller, "I see my father in him every day. And he was his age when his world came apart."

Tears welled in her eyes. She choked back a sob before speaking of the most anguished period of her life. All of us have an inexpressible chapter in our story, one which words fail to describe. Jurema's pain was unfathomable. She spoke of how the calamity came about. Her father had cosigned a loan for his youngest brother. When the brother defaulted, her father had to assume the debt. The country was in a period of economic crisis, and he had no savings. In less than a year he lost everything he had amassed in decades. And that was only the beginning.

"Many lose and start over. My father would have, but in the midst of the crisis he caught my mother in bed with my youngest uncle, the one who had bankrupted him. Maybe because of me or because he loved her so much, I don't know, he didn't leave her. Then some of the men he owed accused him of trying to start a revolt. And that same uncle was in collusion with them. My father was unjustly tried and humiliated. He was imprisoned for a month."

Her father, shamed, withdrew into his quarters and began to suffer panic attacks, screaming as if he were about to die. The doctors couldn't find anything wrong. His insanity grew deeper, and he lost the will to fight.

Her voice faltering, she said that none of his relatives ever came to visit him. His own brothers wouldn't touch him for fear of "catching" his mental illness.

"My hero had become a villain. Finally, something terrible happened. My mother had him committed to an asylum. I was ten years old. They had taken away my foundation, stolen my innocence."

At that moment, Jurema collapsed in sobs. Monica lent her a handkerchief. After regaining composure, Jurema spoke of the core of her pain, the events that had hurt her the most.

"When they were taking him away to the asylum, I heard my father calling my name: 'Juremita! Juremita! Don't let them put me away! I'm not crazy. I love you, help me!' I ran to help him, but my mother and my uncles stopped me. 'It's for his own good, sweetheart,' my mother said, tired of the man she didn't love and who could no longer work. I'm an elderly woman, but to this day I dream about my father calling out to me and asking for help."

The episode had occurred over seventy years ago, but the torment still raged in her mind. All of the dreamseller's followers were moved to learn once again that we didn't really know one another. We discovered that without making an inventory of our histories and sharing it with those we loved, our social relationships were mere theater. We were a group of strangers under the same roof.

Jurema begged her mother to let her visit her father but was told he needed to be isolated. That separation was against all the principles of psychiatry. Little Jurema sent letters almost daily to her father, but they never arrived. Her mother didn't mail them.

After so much pleading, two years, seven months, six days after the commitment, her mother finally gave in and took her to visit him. The girl was perplexed at seeing her father. He was completely different, both physically and intellectually from when he had been taken away. He had been disfigured by mistreatment and by countless electroshock therapies. Weeping, she ran to him and said, "Daddy, Daddy, it's me, your daughter, your Juremita." But he didn't recognize her.

Jurema stared at us and completed her inventory.

"I shouted my father's name, trying to wake him up from his sleep," she said. "Seeing my desperation, a cold, unfeeling, inhumane psychiatrist appeared and told my mother in front of me that my father's illness was genetic in nature and that I stood a good chance of ending up like him. He urged her to find a psychiatrist for me. That's how I grew up, with a ghost haunting me. I grew up thinking that sooner or later I would meet the same fate as my father."

A year later, her father died and was buried. She didn't go to see his body. Many years after she had become a university professor, she decided to study psychopathology and came to understand that her father's illness, panic syndrome, was perfectly treatable. But psychiatry, then in its infancy, committed atrocities.

"I've learned that throughout our lives we must build bridges of pardon, especially to pardon ourselves. Otherwise, we won't survive. I've learned that no mental illness diminishes a human being's dignity. I've learned that to exclude or isolate someone is to kill them emotionally, to murder them without stopping their heartbeats."

The dreamseller stood up and solemnly applauded her. With tears in his eyes, he told her in a soft voice, "You do more than I can ever do. You sell more dreams than I do."

"I need to look upon life as the show of shows and understand that both tears and laughter are privileges of the living," she said. "In the months or years I have left to live, I have to learn to remove the restraints from my mind. To be freer and more flexible, to live more gently and to be more wildly in love with life. And for that I need this band of misfits to help me." And she smiled.

We all ran to embrace her, as did the students of psychology and medicine.

The Mayor told Jurema, "Mommy, I'm going to kiss you. You're beautiful." And he kissed her several times on the forehead. She tried to escape, asking the others for help.

Once things had calmed down, Honeymouth added, "Mommy, if you become mentally ill, I want you to know that there are two perfectly healthy men here who invented the revolutionary scream therapy. No mental demon can withstand our technique."

"I'm going to scream, all right," she said. "But to get away from you, you scoundrel."

We all laughed. Then, we danced and sang, and made fun of one another. We have all experienced tragedy, but we have found shelter in each other.

CHAPTER 27

Ghosts That Must Be Tamed

PROFESSOR JUREMA'S INVENTORY WAS A BALM THAT salved our stories. We discovered that it is possible to transform our arid mental terrain into a blooming garden like the one we were in that day.

For years I studied the human condition in sociology books, but it never entered my mind that heaven and hell, comfort and pain, were very close at hand. I never imagined that it was so difficult, yet so easy, to share some of our secrets. I never realized that it was so complex, but at the same time so simple, to built bridges, to connect the islands in our minds.

After that solemn celebration we were at the height of joy. No one had gone to Disney World, yet none of us had ever had so much fun. No one had gone to the movies, yet we never experienced such emotion. No one went to a psychotherapy session, yet no psychotherapy ever had such an effect on us. No one went to school, yet we had never learned as much.

We sat in a circle, awaiting the dreamseller's latest words. He breathed several long, satisfied sighs. He sold dreams of a free history, one that reunites its fragments, binds up its wounds, breaks the chains, and lets air flow into every corner of its vaults. That was the dream of Buddha, Confucius,

Socrates, Plato and the other great thinkers. It was the dream of the teacher of teachers, the man born in Nazareth.

"It's refreshing to take off our makeup and be what we always were: human beings, silly and lucid, incoherent and wise, fragile and secure—in short, paradoxical. Whoever doesn't invent his story doesn't rewrite his texts. Remember, every human being either has his ghosts or constructs them.

"I cry when I think that from preschool to university we're creating children who don't know how to delve into their minds. They're like houses built on foundations of misinformation. When storms strike, they have no shutters to protect themselves, no emotional filter to help them survive."

Unlike many masters of past and present, the dreamseller was selling motivational words. He didn't talk about a victorious life crowned by success. For him, existence was a contract of risk. And the clauses in that contract contained every part of man's story: stress and peace of mind, tears and laughter, madness and sanity. It is in that whirlwind that his lessons emerge.

He was an honest man, more honest than any mental health professional I ever met. He sold dreams of a free mind, but that freedom had to be won amid our ghosts and through intellectual sweat. As if examining his own history and plunging into his own inventory, he told us a story.

"Even a well-to-do person without financial ghosts can be tormented by social ghosts: betrayal, disappointments, offenses, slander, loss. Even if he has no social ghosts, he can be disturbed by mental phantoms: guilt, anguish, an inferiority complex, shyness, obsessions, bitter mental images. And even if he has no mental phantoms he can be unnerved by existential ghosts: death, transcendence, the lack of meaning in life. And even if he has no existential ghosts he may worry about the frailty of his body, fatigue, headaches, muscular pains, sleeplessness, nightmares."

And, intently observing his listeners, he stated, "The great human challenge is not to eliminate the ghosts we have created but to tame them. I say this because we possess surprising creativity."

Yes, it's true, we see problems where none exist. His ideas, cutting but at the same time gentle, reverberated in the hundred billion neurons of our brains.

"I know my project of selling dreams generates both admiration and scandal," he said. "Some call me a lunatic, others an impostor, still others a heretic, a deceiver, an instigator. But when I look over the inventory of my ghosts, when I review the traumas I've been through, the monsters in the present shrink and those in the future no longer frighten me. The bridges between my past, my present and expectations for the future bring me peace."

The psychology students had the privilege of hearing ideas that would mark their story. They understood that if they didn't recognize their ghosts and their troubles, they would have limited ability to treat the ghosts of others. I saw that young Solomon was fascinated by what he had heard, but also tense.

"I have ghosts that terrify me, Julio Cesar," he told me.

"So do I, my young friend. But we can't give in to them."

Just when everything was flowing smoothly, once again the pair of agitators stepped in to stir things up. Barnabas said, "Voters of this great city: I pledge that if elected mayor I will put all the people's ghosts in jail. There won't be a single one left to haunt you."

"The Mayor is a demagogue. Look at me! I'm a professional ghost hunter. I have experience!" Bartholomew said, cutting in.

The Mayor reached into his pocket and took out a stuffed toy mouse that he'd found in the trash and kept for just such an occasion. Tying it onto a string, he dangled it in front of Bartholomew, and something incredible happened: Bartholomew, faced with that tiny animal, went into a panic. We couldn't believe that the invincible and unstoppable Honeymouth harbored a ghost we were unaware of: a phobia of rats.

Bartholomew squealed like a schoolgirl and jumped into Crusher's lap. The philosophic atmosphere of that great inventory came crashing down. But on the other hand, I loved seeing the egomaniacal Honeymouth humbled by a mouse. We never laughed so much. It was like getting our revenge.

The Mayor continued his joke, trying to place the small inanimate mouse in Honeymouth's hands. The dreamseller took advantage of that moment to teach us: "Ghosts appear when we fail to distinguish fantasy from reality."

We saw Bartholomew shivering and cringing. It wasn't appropriate to laugh; after all, it was one of his fears. But because he made fun of everyone, even at the most inopportune moments, we couldn't hold back our laughter. For the first time, I assisted in turning drama into comedy.

"The great orator, the dragon slayer, in panic over a little mouse," I said, getting even.

Embarrassed, but without losing his poise as a street philosopher, he climbed out of Crusher's arms, "dusted" his pants and shirt, and answered, "Julio Cesar, noted emperor of the madhouse of society, knows that every great man has his secrets."

CHAPTER 28

Demons Island

J UST AS WE WERE JOKING ABOUT BARTHOLOMEW'S GHOSTS, Fernando Lataro, the warden of the maximum security prison, came closer. He was astonished at what he had seen and heard. Before taking part in the experiment of the historical inventories, he had felt that his institution was society's sewer, the end of the line, a warehouse for brutal criminals and incorrigible sociopaths.

That institution was notorious for its violence and uprisings, its drug traffic and riots. It was on an island some thirty miles from the coast, nicknamed "Demons Island" because it housed the country's most dangerous men. Since he had taken over its administration two years earlier, five uprisings had occurred, resulting in the deaths of three guards, one administrator and ten prisoners.

Life had no value to the majority of those prisoners. They had committed unimaginable atrocities. Some had killed their wives, others their parents, and still others their children. Some were kidnappers, bank robbers and drug traffickers. Others were terrorists and Mafiosi who thought another person's life wasn't worth more than a bullet.

Working on Demons Island meant facing a different kind of ghost. The clergy wouldn't dare visit. Musicians wouldn't play there. Philanthropists pretended the institution didn't exist. No one would take a chance. The turnover of guards, social workers, psychologists and educators was staggering. Some fell ill the first month there. Every year, half the employees requested medical leave, with real justification.

I knew Demons Island and its reputation better than most. In the past, I had asked my students to do sociological research into the perspective of those criminals. They were unsuccessful. They were threatened and thrown out by the inmates, some of whom commanded gangs from inside. My students feared being threatened by their accomplices on the outside. Cocaine, heroin, pot and hallucinogens would frequently get past the institution's rigorous security checks.

The warden and his staff were desperate over the prisoners' recent actions. They suspected an escape was being planned. The warden himself, three guards and five educators had received death threats. They had to have bodyguards, even outside the prison. "Violence has reached unimaginable levels," the warden told us, concerned. "It's not just the socially underprivileged youths or ones with serious family problems who are perpetrating criminal acts. Now, young people from the middle class are committing atrocities against innocent people. In many schools, violence has become routine. I don't understand it." And, remembering the dreamseller's words from an earlier occasion, he added, "We've made breakthroughs in technology, but in terms of altruism and tolerance we're in our infancy."

Following his brief account, the dispirited warden made a request of the dreamseller that shook me:

"Master, I was moved by your technique of making an inventory of the five greatest dramas in our history. Do you think you and your disciples could teach it to the inmates in my institution? At least to some of them? Maybe they'd have a chance to develop some spark of sensitivity and social responsibility."

I thought, "Is that even possible? Who could make those psychopaths look inside themselves? It's an extremely risky, extremely dangerous experiment. How would we get them to see the importance of sharing their story with others, when they kill without hesitation?" One of the Demons Island staff was more incisive.

"Society treats our inmates like garbage," he said, "and those of us who work there have to endure them. Despite their crimes, they're human beings. Can't you please try to help us?"

Of course, I never expected the dreamseller to accept. For one thing, his life had already been in jeopardy recently. Surely he wouldn't want to expose himself to this kind of risk, much less expose his vulnerable disciples. But before he declined, Honeymouth answered for the dreamseller and the rest of us.

"Count us in! We'll teach those boys a lesson or two."

"A few raps on the knuckles and everything'll be fine," the Mayor joked.

They didn't know what they were talking about. But before I could contradict them, the warden and his workers applauded. "Bravo! Thank you so much!"

Bartholomew and Barnabas, naïve as they were, thought the institution was a public school with some unruly students. They had no idea what Demons Island was like. They'd be eaten alive the first time they opened their mouths to crack a joke.

"At last, noted thinkers are going to invest in Demons Island," an equally naïve guard said.

"Thinkers?" I asked myself silently. "They only think about nonsense."

"Educate the young and prisons will become museums," the Mayor said.

This time the dreamseller became very pensive, barely breathing. He knew the terrain he had been invited to tread.

"You've just accepted a mission to perform in a maximum security prison," the dreamseller told the two showoffs.

Honeymouth realized what he'd done. With a lump in his throat he asked, "Maximum security prison, master?"

"Yes, and if you really want to, this is an opportunity to sell dreams in a setting where it's almost impossible to dream," the dreamseller said calmly after a long pause.

Fernando Lataro brightened up.

"I'll provide all the security we have at our disposal," he told us.

Bartholomew, trying to come up with an excuse to get out of the mission, turned to Barnabas: "Mayor, I can see you look tired, unsteady on your feet. Maybe we should . . ."

"No, I'm fine. Ready for anything." Then he caught on and corrected himself, "Oh, I mean, uh . . . no, I'm not fine. I'm going through male menopause."

But it was too late. The dreamseller had taken a liking to the project.

"Why don't you put on a show about Bartholomew's rat phobia for those prisoners and use that to explain the formation of emotional phantoms?" he told them. "After all, we all have some rats in our mental cellars. Maybe Julio Cesar could direct the skit."

"Excellent idea! Maybe we can do some cleaning up in those criminals' lairs using the story of this complicated human being," the Mayor said, pointing to Honeymouth.

"My people, this man, alias the Mayor, is an example of a poor wretch who had every opportunity to turn down the wrong path. And in the end he did . . ," Honeymouth said. And he burst into laughter. Then, seeing the Mayor's reaction, he corrected himself. "But because he's learning to tame his unruly ghosts he's still got a chance." And he laughed again.

The pair joked about everything and everyone, and at the

most inappropriate times. But they were so amusing that it was virtually impossible not to laugh at them. Some smiled without having the slightest idea what awaited us. But I turned to Jurema and whispered, "Do you know what Demons Island is?"

"Yes. We'll be roasted on a spit," she hissed under her breath. "And anyone who gets out alive will probably have a target on his back!"

Monica overheard the conversation and shuddered. The professor was well acquainted with the notorious institution. She had sent some of her students to try to work with the inmates. But nothing was effective. Her students left there almost stripped bare.

Seeing how risky the mission was, I drew back: "Master, forgive me, but I'm out! It's too risky. Wandering about with Bartholomew and Barnabas is one thing, but working with them to educate the offenders on Demons Island is insanity."

"Well, look here, everyone. The great educator is scared of his students."

And to my amazement, a med student, John Vitor, a drug user who had cried on my shoulder several times in recent weeks, said, "Why not? I'm game to help them, too. I've been in jail myself."

John Vitor was nearly expelled from college. He had injected cocaine, and his veins had hardened from shooting up daily. In desperation, he started in on his hands and feet. I saw my son John Marcus in John Vitor. Similar names with similar stories. But after walking with the dreamseller the last two months, he had begun to reorganize his story.

I first met John Vitor when I found him convulsing from an overdose. I panicked, thinking he was going to die in my arms. I came to invest in the young man with every fiber of my being. We would meet under the bridges where he slept. Once we talked from eight at night until four in the morning.

I was happy to see him recover, and I began to dream that he might become one of the dreamseller's disciples. I knew it wouldn't erase his past as an addict, but it could help him form a new future. But this mission was very risky. And John Vitor's time in jail for small amounts of drug possession couldn't prepare him for the institution that Fernando Lataro ran.

There were other drugs users who followed the dreamseller. Little by little they learned it was possible to inject adventures into their veins without using drugs of any kind; walking with Bartholomew and Barnabas apparently was enough. But the adventure to Demons Island seemed destined to fail.

I didn't want to disappoint John Vitor, but I was reluctant, even after the warden's guarantees. I had to reveal that I cared about people's pain. I had to abandon my status as intellectual and show my humanity. But I hesitated.

I shook my head. Monica, Solomon, Dima and Edson, who were more daring than I, urged me on. Then, Bartholomew challenged me.

"If the great Julio Cesar directs the play, I'll give an unforgettable performance!"

"Yes! If the emperor of the theatrical arts directs me, I'll set that institution of pampered men on fire!" said the Mayor.

Still unsure, I decided to accept the challenge. And as soon as I did, I suddenly had a flash. I thought: "This is my great chance to get even with these miserable gasbags. They've put me down, made me the butt of jokes, but now they'll pay."

"Okay, I accept," I said, to the applause of the crowd. "I'll write the script and cast the characters in incredible roles."

They were all happy. They carried me off on their shoulders. They had fallen into my trap. But deep down, I was afraid of falling into a trap of my own.

CHAPTER 29

Threatened on Demons Island

To WRITE THE SCRIPT FOR THE PLAY WE WOULD PUT ON AT Demons Island, I listened attentively to some of the periods in Bartholomew's life and the reason that rat trauma haunted him like a ghost. The loudmouth talked and exaggerated, and I furiously took notes. I had to have the patience of Job. As I was writing the script, I prepared small traps for both the street philosopher and the barroom politician.

As I structured their characters, I thought they'd be eaten alive by the audience of criminals. Of course, I didn't want things to get out of hand, but I confess I dreamed of teaching them an unforgettable lessons. It was my opportunity to take the place of the dreamseller and educate those insubordinate and uncontrollable disciples in my own way. I knew I committed many errors as an educator, but my authoritarian instinct was aroused, my claws emerged from my unconscious and came into play at the conscious level.

It was one thing to write the script; rehearsing was another. They wouldn't memorize the text, they improvised dialogue, and joked around too much. We rehearsed under bridges, in squares, on the streets.

"Director, I'm surprising myself," said Honeymouth, patting himself on the back. "I've discovered I'm a very talented actor."

"If directors in Hollywood discover me, I'll take my place alongside Tom Cruise and Chaplin," said the Mayor.

"Chaplin's been dead for a long time," Solomon said.

"Dead? Well, not in my heart, Solomon," he replied, craftily extricating himself.

After rehearsing for a week, we took a ferry to the infamous Demons Island. All the closest disciples were present, including the beautiful Monica. Although we recommended she stay behind because of the unforeseeable risks she would run from being exposed to those sexually deprived men, she insisted on going. The boat was an old modified ferry, a hundred feet long, with wooden seats. Its white paint was faded and its tired motors growled. There were five guards on board.

The wind swept our hair into our eyes, producing a pleasant sensation. The breeze from the sea perfumed our nostrils and cleared away the fetid odors of gloomy bridges. It was shaping up to be a memorable day. And it was. Unaware of what awaited him, Bartholomew said, "Ah! I love being pampered."

"I'm gonna make the audience cry," said the Mayor.

The helmsman, hearing this, shook his head and said, "Everybody leaving this damned island cries, my friends."

I had a lump in my throat. The grind of rehearsals clouded my consciousness, narrowing my perception: we were going not to a theater but to a slaughterhouse. My heart shuddered at seeing the island in the distance. I suspect tears actually rolled down my cheeks. I turned toward the small port from which we had departed and brushed the hair out of my eyes to see the continent to which we were saying farewell. I wondered if I would ever set foot there again.

I was never an optimistic man. Pessimism is in fact the favorite diet of most intellectuals. Optimism, we often think, is something for stupid people alienated from reality. But that day I had concrete reasons for wallowing. I had a feeling that my plans weren't going to work out. As we approached the island, my heart and lungs lost their serenity, accelerated, begging for a way out. I asked myself, "What was I thinking when I agreed to do this?"

There were no beaches on Demons Island, just cliffs rising more than thirty feet into the air. The waves crashed violently against the rocks, producing a deafening roar. That funereal landscape, devoid of life, revealed a devastated coastal vegetation like the souls on that rock.

The prison was surrounded by a stone wall forty-five feet high. At one time, this had been a holding area for political prisoners. Later, the imposing structure was turned into the most respected and feared maximum security facility in the country.

As we entered the prison, we were subjected to a thorough inspection. Five men searched us. We were racked with fear as we approached the inmate area. If the landscape outside the walls was unusual, the inside was caustic. Small gardens with badly tended grass. There were no flowers, no trees, no beauty. Worn walls, faded paint and holes in the narrow streets contributed to the image of punishment. It was one more sentence imposed on those dangerous offenders. Their dream was not to pay their debt to society but to flee the chaos. Atop the wall, men with machine guns patrolled, knowing that sooner or later another riot would break out.

Many of the prisoners were serving life sentences. Killing or dying made little difference to those whose hopes had been exhausted. As we headed to the amphitheater, we passed through an immense central courtyard with cells on both sides. Only a few criminals were "free" in the courtyard. Some were there for good behavior, others through bribery and still others to keep down internal tension. Those who were loose were exercising under strict supervision. I felt a chill from their hateful stares.

A criminal with tattoos on his shoulders and chest shouted to his comrades, "They're visiting us like you visit animals in the zoo." And he imitated various animals, from elephants to lions.

Professor Jurema lost her balance and became dizzy. Dimas, a specialist in petty theft, seemed like a defenseless infant compared to the capacity for evil of those men. Solomon was feverish and sweating. Edson's lips were trembling, and he was praying under his breath to ward off the specter of panic. Crusher was silent. John Vitor went pale and regretted having encouraged me to accept the challenge. I couldn't read Monica's reaction, for she had had to wear an unkempt wig and baggy clothes to conceal her curves.

Honeymouth and the Mayor were, as always, on another planet. They swaggered like a couple of playboys, as if commanding a battalion. They were ten yards ahead of the group, with three unarmed guards, as guns were forbidden in the courtyard. Wherever they went, they waved, greeted, said hello, exactly as they did with strangers when they were in the streets.

One psychopath, in a cell to the right some twelve yards away, seeing them moving so casually in his territory, became irritated. He spat on the ground toward them. The pair spat right back. I don't know whether they were trying to provoke him or to show they were his equal.

A murderer who had wiped out a family of five, seeing the Mayor blissfully gobbling down crackers, shouted, "Get ready to go on a diet, fatso. You're gonna lose a hundred pounds."

"Fantastic! That's my dream, big guy," the Mayor replied insolently.

But I sensed that he was starting to feel shaken. His politician's spirit began cooling off. Ten paces ahead, a kidnapper

insulted Honeymouth. Amid laughter from his companions, he
bellowed, "Where ya goin', baby? C'mere, sweetheart."

I thought that this time Honeymouth would keep quiet, but
to our amazement he stole a glance at the guards walking beside him and reacted. "That's it! Hold me back!" And he raised
his fists.

The prisoners went wild, trying to break through the bars.
I froze and my lips started to quiver.

Tensely, the guard advised him, "Listen, anybody who
can't take an insult in here ends up sleeping in the cemetery."

Honeymouth swallowed hard, and his bravado subsided.
He and Barnabas opened up more space between us and them;
fear quickens one's steps. The dreamseller was walking uncon-
cerned at our side. I couldn't understand where that calm came
from. But even calm men have a limit; the dreamseller was no
different. It wouldn't be long before I saw him shaken.

CHAPTER 30

Conspiracy

A MAN NICKNAMED "EL DIABLO," WHO HAD A SHAVED HEAD and scars on both cheeks, was sitting on a bench in the courtyard, near another criminal nicknamed "Shrapnel." El Diablo and Shrapnel were dangerous terrorists, gang bosses and leaders at the prison. They were feared and dictated the "honor code," ordering hits on people inside and outside Demons Island. Each of them was serving several life sentences for their crimes, not to mention the crimes for which they were still waiting to be tried. They were in the courtyard because of their power. Fernando Lataro felt it best to allow them a few privileges rather than have them incite the beasts and start a rebellion—a dangerous tactic of dubious value.

El Diablo rose from the bench and stared at length at the dreamseller. Shrapnel did the same. Slowly, they approached. In addition to the guards accompanying Bartholomew and Barnabas, four more were at our side. The guards began to get nervous at their approach. If they gave the signal, an armed guard would lock his rifle on the courtyard. But the terrorists made no aggressive moves. El Diablo was astonished at the sight of the dreamseller. Like the director of the Mellon Lincoln Hospital, Lucio Lobo, he looked as if he'd seen a ghost.

When he was six feet away from the dreamseller, he said

vehemently, "It's not possible! You're alive! Are you here for revenge?"

For the first time, I saw the dreamseller puzzled. He didn't understand. Revenge was not a word in his dictionary. He lived the art of tolerance. Surely the criminal was confused, I thought.

"Revenge? The best revenge against an enemy is to forgive him," the dreamseller said.

"You're full of it! You wouldn't forgive your executioners. You came here for revenge. But you won't get out of here alive." And he threatened to lunge at the dreamseller. We were on edge. Fortunately, other guards with weapons showed up and calmed matters.

"Can't you see he's a beggar?" said one of the guards, trying to calm the aggressor's anger.

I was distressed. In recent weeks the dreamseller had faced two assassination attempts. For whom was he being mistaken? Every theater director has moments of insecurity when he begins a new season, but I would have given anything in my power to resign from the job.

We were quickly brought to the backstage area of the amphitheater. Bartholomew and Barnabas were already there. But no one was able to concentrate. This was going to be a fiasco. We wouldn't even be able to speak the lines, much less act them out. Worse, we would probably spark a riot. Later we learned that some of the leaders, including the members of the Chinese Mafia, were planning to use the event to attempt to escape in the boat in which we'd come.

The day of the event, Fernando Lataro got word of the escape plan and, instead of canceling it thought it best to make a show of force by setting up a comprehensive security plan. He didn't want to add to the prisoners' dissatisfaction since our performance had been announced for over a week. In addition, he wanted the worst criminals to be present in order to better keep an eye on them. And he dreamed that the technique of making a historical inventory might produce some effect on his "clientele."

Little by little, the amphitheater began to fill up. The criminals were grumbling. We could hear some of the cursing:

"Let's get this piece of crap started!"

"Theater is for little girls!"

"Open that goddamn curtain right now!"

Hearing the insults and knowing we were on a powder keg, I began having hot flashes like a woman in menopause; at the same time, my mind froze. I couldn't think. There were thirty heavily armed guards in the side hallways. The dreamseller, the warden, three staff members, two social workers and a psychologist were sitting in the front row, on the left side. El Diablo and Shrapnel, along with the other crime leaders, were in the front row on the right side.

The criminals began raising the level of their threats:

"If I don't like it, I'm gonna kill one of 'em," El Diablo shouted angrily, drawing applause from the audience.

"If I don't like it, I'm gonna eat all the actors' livers," snarled Shrapnel.

They were enraged because this play had foiled their initial plan to riot against the guards that day. As our play dealt with the construction of ghosts of the mind, I thought that the mere staging by the actors wouldn't be sufficient to explain the concept. I felt a narrator was necessary and cast myself in that role. I would therefore have to go onstage before the actors, pick up the microphone and give succinct explanations of the progress of the piece. I began to realize that I had been caught in my own trap.

Seeing my hesitation behind the curtain, the Mayor shoved

me through, and I suddenly found myself onstage. I dropped
the cordless microphone. They started booing and shouting
nonstop. "Get going, dumbass."

Trying to regain my composure, I remembered the days
when my students, shivering in fear, would remain deadly
silent. So I raised my voice and began the greetings. But the
only authority these criminals respected were revolvers and
machine guns.

"I'd like to thank Warden Fernando Lataro for the invitation."

As soon as I mentioned the warden's name, they roared
like predators facing an easy prey. They seemed to have a Plan
B. They would confront the guards, and even if some of them
were shot, they would overpower them and take control of
their weapons. It would be a disaster. They had committed serious crimes and possessed the biological tools for survival on
that wretched island, but their intellectual, emotional and cul-
tural tools were crushed. They were frayed, frustrated human
beings who felt like rats in a sewer.

Terrified, I tried praising the participants in order to reduce
the tension.

"Esteemed spectators, it is an honor—" Hearing this, they
shouted:

"Enough of this garbage!"

Others yelled, "Lets trash the place."

Desperate, I immediately proceeded to the objective. "I'd
like to tell you about this story."

But no one was interested in hearing about or seeing any
play.

"Stupid intellectual. Kiss ass!"

In anguish, my voice catching in my throat, I looked to the
dreamseller to see if I could borrow some of his energy. But I

saw nothing. My heart was racing so fast that you could see it moving under my polo shirt. I wanted to be anywhere else in the world but there. All my knowledge of violence and criminality turned to dust. The worst criminals in the country were prisoners behind bars made of steel, and I was behind bars of panic. We were all prisoners, and all of us wanted to flee.

CHAPTER 31

Shocking the Psychopaths and Murderers

W ORRIED ABOUT A PRISON RIOT, FERNANDO LATARO TRIED to assert his authority as warden. He climbed onto the stage and asked for respect. Instead of heeding him, the inmates rose and started toward the stage. The whole place was charged. I didn't know whether to run away or stand my ground. The uproar had become unsustainable. Just as the guards were about to attack the criminals, a phantom applied a 10,000 volt shock to all present: It was Bartholomew.

He came onto the stage so quickly and screamed so loud that I almost had a heart attack. The warden was startled. The audience, taken by surprise, took a second to process the hurricane that had just been unleashed.

He wore a wig whose strands stood straight up and out to the sides like something from a horror film. It was Monica's wig. He was dressed in a navy blue blouse, a skirt and jacket and high heels. The clothes were from another era, lent by Jurema. He, or rather "she," was so ugly that not even the most perverted men in the prison could be turned on by the sight. Then the Mayor came on stage wearing a blond wig, emitting primitive sounds along with Honeymouth and thrashing about. They were performing scream therapy onstage.

Witnessing the performance of those two, I was all but beside myself. What were they up to? If anything, I was sure
they'd fuel the riot. They had no idea what they were getting
into. I had visions of the predators in the audience tearing them
limb from limb.

El Diablo and Shrapnel, seeing their comrades distracted by
the two crazies, snorted in rage. They looked at all the posted
guards and, just as they were about to give the order to start
the uprising, Bartholomew and the Mayor went right up to
them. They removed their wigs, threw them onto the floor in
anger, and crossed their fingers. I thought they were making
the sign of the cross because they felt they were going to die.

El Diablo and Shrapnel, when they saw them, were stunned.
They immediately took a step back, confused. The criminals
seemed to be waiting for a cue from them for how to react.

Just then, someone turned down the house lights. Seeing that
calm was being reestablished, instead of also quieting down and
going backstage, Bartholomew and the Mayor donned their wigs
again and began to imitate various animals, from bears to di-
nosaurs. And they were actually good at it. They looked like a
couple of crazy people having a psychotic break.

Fernando Lataro sat down again. He was as lost as the prisoners. Maybe the play's already started, he thought. But all of
that had been improvised. Some of the prisoners began laughing at our misfits. Suddenly, the "loonies" stopped. An absolute
silence fell over the theater. Creepy music, like something out
of a Hitchcock film, began to play.

Honeymouth walked slowly to center stage, staring at the
audience in silence, as if about to devour them with his eyes.
He then emitted a sound as though his heart was exploding.
And he collapsed onto the floor. He hit his forehead against
the platform and lay there, still. The psychopaths, murderers,

kidnappers, terrorists and rapists looked at one another and wondered what it meant.

Then the Mayor, who had sneaked backstage, appeared with a coffin on his shoulders, material he had requested without my knowledge from one of the staff members. His appearance was horrifying. He placed Bartholomew in the coffin. Then he raised his head and, eyes wide as if he were the main character in a horror movie, said in a haunting voice: "I am death." And, pointing to the audience, shouted, "I'm going to eat your brain, rip apart your thoughts." With a terrifying laugh, he said, "I am death, hahahaha! I destroy the powerful, crush psychopaths, hahahaha!"

At that instant, the stage lights dimmed even further, imparting more tension to the scene. The Mayor took a knife from inside his shirt, kneeled beside the coffin and stabbed Honeymouth, moving as if he were cutting open his brain. I was truly frightened. It looked so real . . . Moments later, after smearing himself with "blood," he yanked something from his friend. I was close to four yards away and almost fainted when I saw what it was.

"I've got his braaaaaain!" he screamed, as if holding up a trophy. It looked like an actual brain. And, as incredible as it seems, he began to eat it and smear himself with blood.

"I love killers' brain," said the Mayor, howling with delight and fear.

I was so stunned by what I was seeing. While he spoke, strange sounds came from behind the scenes, making the horror scene seem more realistic.

I stole a glance at the audience, now in rapt attention. An instant earlier we were on the verge of being lynched; now the prisoners seemed like helpless little boys. Some had their hands on their head, trying to protect their skull. For the first time, the criminals felt like victims of fear. But I was afraid that if anything disturbed the atmosphere of tension, it would be shattered and the rebellion would begin.

The Mayor presented himself as the psychopath to end all psychopaths. He invaded the prisoners' minds uninvited. El Diablo was dismayed; he couldn't take his eyes off the old coffin. Reflecting, he understood that one day he would face a phantom from which he could not defend himself: his own death. Like virtually every violent man, he avoided thinking about it with all his might. But now he was forced to think that everything he loved, everything he had fought for, everything he had aspired to would crumble in a tiny tomb. He would become nothing, simply nothing.

The dreamseller watched a small sample of the revolution of the anonymous take shape on stage. The Mayor rose beside the coffin and proclaimed:

"Silence! I am going to speak of the most conspiratorial theory in existence. A theory that would baffle Einstein, destroy this prison and make agent 007 shudder!"

A theory? What did he have up his sleeve? Many of the prisoners didn't even know what a theory was. At most they'd had a few years of schooling. But none had ever cracked a book or learned even the simplest arithmetic. How could they understand a theory?

Then the Mayor approached the silent audience, which was intently following every move, and bellowed, "The theory of the flatus!"

"Flatus?" said warden Fernando Lataro, extremely concerned.

"Flatus?" the dreamseller wondered aloud.

"Theory of what?" everyone asked. No one laughed; the atmosphere they had created was so tense that no one imagined what that theory could mean. Perhaps it dealt with a chemical weapon, or a new rocket fuel. But suddenly, to our relief, Bartholomew got out of the coffin, the stage lights went up, and circus music began to play!

The general sentiment shifted from terror to comedy. My mind did flip-flops. So did the prisoners'. Even those men, accustomed to the risk of death, of being mutilated and imprisoned, weren't prepared for such an abrupt change. For several seconds they didn't know whether to laugh or cry.

Even the dreamseller appeared confused. All he knew was that those two irrepressible characters stunned this crowd. I began to imagine that maybe Bartholomew and Barnabas knew those criminals better than any policeman or forensic psychiatrist. Maybe they represented a greater danger to society than the offenders on Demons Island.

When the lights went up, the pair was wearing clown noses and top hats. The audience applauded them, and then the Mayor spoke of his "complex" theory. Once again, I nearly fainted.

The Mayor turned his considerable backside to the audience and said:

"Distinguished public, whoever understands the theory of the flatus will never again look upon his buttocks the same way." And the Mayor let loose a thunderclap that shook the amphitheater. At that moment everyone understood what the theory of the flatus was.

The audience erupted in laughter. Everyone went from experiencing the height of tension to the height of release. One moment their brains were swallowed up in a coffin, the next they were farting like school kids. My head started to hurt. Clinging to my theories, I asked myself: What happened to the pedagogical atmosphere? What about teaching the historical inventory?

The dreamseller brought his hands up to his face. I didn't know if he was enjoying himself or if he wanted to run away.

But he seemed to be smiling. I didn't know whether the pair had created this Plan B with his consent or whether everything was improvised, as always. I didn't know anything. I was totally uninformed, the last to know what was happening.

The warden was apprehensive, thinking that this time the circus really was about to catch on fire. The guards in the corridors were of two minds, some were relaxing and smiling, others were fearing the worst and grasping their weapons. Suddenly, another character appeared on stage to perform with the two buffoons and explain that wackiest of all theories: Professor Jurema. I couldn't imagine that a brilliant intellectual like her would get mixed up in this craziness.

"My children, the air is democratic. It belongs to all and must be cared for by all," she told the offenders. "Defendants release flatuses, policemen release flatuses and so do intellectuals. It's one way we're all the same. No one is exempt: babies, children, adults, the elderly, celebrities, the anonymous, rich, poor—in short, everyone farts. The only ones who don't are dead," and she pointed to the coffin.

"Every human being releases ten thousand flatuses during his lifetime, increasing the greenhouse effect. We are all 'farters,'" said Honeymouth and the Mayor in unison.

"There are several varieties of flatuses," said Professor Jurema.

And the two rowdies began explaining the famous types.

"There's the psychopathic farter," said the Mayor. "The psychopath comes along all sweet and light, nice as can be, and when everyone least expects it, it erupts like a silent torpedo that sinks the victim."

Next, Honeymouth explained the "Judas flatus."

"It's the most treacherous of them all. You trust that flatus, believe it's your best friend and think it'll never betray you. You take a deep breath, pray for it to come out quietly and not give you away. But suddenly, when you least expect it, the Judas comes out like screeching tires. And you innocently say something like 'I think it's going to rain today,' but everybody knows it was you who broke the thunder."

I looked at the prisoners and saw them cracking up. It was hard to believe that those men were the most violent members of society. I thought to myself, "Every human being, whether a criminal or a victim, is hungry and thirsty for laughter." Freud was right when he said that the pleasure principle rules the human mind.

Honeymouth continued effusively:

"There's the socialite flatus. Imagine three high-society women friends meeting. Each of them wearing dark glasses bigger than their heads. One of them looses a subtle flatus, inaudible. And has the gall to say, 'I think there's something rotten in here.'"

"Dear listeners, there's also the intellectual flatus," bellowed the Mayor, looking at me. "That's the most shameless of all. The guy knows the flatus is at the doorway of—of making its escape." And he looked at Professor Jurema, who approved the pedagogical language.

"Yes, the gases are at the doorway, and he releases them without a second thought. The intellectual subtly goes on talking like nothing happened."

The inmates were enjoying themselves like children. They didn't even seem to be aware that they were in a maximum security prison. At that moment, I sidled over to Jurema and whispered, "What about teaching them Piaget? And Vigotski? And Morin?"

"My boy, what are we to do? Even Marx would be lost with these lunatics," she said. "Educating isn't the art of transmitting ideas, it's the art of making them understandable. Those criminals are fed up with advice and sermons. Bartholomew and Barnabas captivated them." And, criticizing me, she added, "Get out of your head, and let yourself go!"

I had a revelation. I had never succeed in reaching my students, never used their own language. I felt that descending from my pedestal and entering their world was too high a price. While I was pondering these things, the Mayor, seeing the crowd delirious with his teachings, went into a trance. His politician's spirit reemerged.

"Citizens of this great institution, hear my platform for the next election. It is based on a simple truth: *No one is worthy of his ass, unless he acknowledges his flatuses!* If every voter who breaks wind votes for me, it'll be the biggest landslide in history!"

After the presentation the three bowed before the audience, along with those who had been working behind the scenes. Later I found out it was John Vitor, Dimas, Solomon and Edson who were controlling the lighting and sound. They were part of Plan B, and I became a mere spectator.

It goes without saying that they brought down the house. For the first time in its centuries of existence, Demons Island became Angels Island, at least for a few hours.

The criminals remained on their feet, applauding the troupe. I stood awkwardly to one side and applauded them as well. They had managed to do what no psychiatrist, psychologist, educator or sociologist had ever done in that institution. When one has a free mind, it's possible to think about other ways of educating.

CHAPTER 32

My Script, Finally

AFTER RAISING A HULLABALOO, MY FRIENDS RETURNED TO their place behind the scenes and I took to the stage. It was my turn to act as narrator of the script I had originally written. A hellish task. But I was more relaxed now. I vowed not to remain indifferent to their misery.

Before beginning my narration, I looked at those men who behaved like teenagers and saw them as little boys whose childhoods had been stolen. Yes, they were responsible for their acts, guilty of their crimes, but they had shattered backgrounds. How could we expect serenity from them if aggression was the pen with which they wrote the fundamental chapters of their story?

I went to center stage. I didn't need to raise my voice or exert any kind of pressure. They had simply quieted down, awaiting my words. I quickly explained that I would be the narrator of the story. The curtains closed, and Bartholomew and the others began their preparations. I asked the spectators to pay close attention to the movements of the characters and to try to understand how easy it is to cause traumas. And I asked a question to wake them up.

"If overprotective parents can traumatize their children, can you imagine what the absence of parents or the presence

of violent or neglectful parents can mean to a child? We're
not trying to justify our mistakes but to show how our ghosts
emerge."

The curtains opened and the spectators smiled in excite-
ment. Bartholomew, dressed as a woman, was reading a magazine. His name was Clotilde. He was wearing a wig even
weirder than the first. The Mayor, whose name in the play was
Romeo, was Clotilde's spouse. That was my bit of revenge in
the script. The two would be ridiculed mercilessly. Married for
ten years, they were irritable, ill-tempered and highly critical
of each other. They represented Bartholomew's parents in the
first years of his life, before his father died and his mother left
him in an orphanage.

Romeo was a TV addict, constantly complaining about the
government. Jurema, Clotilde's mother, was perverse, slovenly
and insane. Clotilde was a professional at embroidery—and
gossip. Dimas and Solomon played the couple's two children,
ages two and five. The rest of the team worked backstage man-
aging the sound.

I began to narrate the story.

"Imagine that in the living room of a modern family, a won-
derful, beautiful woman is reading a fashion magazine." The
audience whistled at Clotilde. Excited, she leafed through the
magazine from back to front and from bottom to top. And, ad-
libbing, proclaimed loudly, "Lovely! Lovely! Ah, this model
looks just like me!"

"Imagine," I said, continuing, "that the magazine shows
nothing but photos of very thin models, undernourished and
sick by medical standards. The more Clotilde reads the magazine, the 'smarter' she becomes," I joked.

I asked them to continue freeing their imagination.

"In that same living room, a father is watching a cop show."
I pointed to Romeo. "The kind of crummy show where every-

body knows ahead of time what's going to happen. There's a good guy and a bad guy. The good guy needs to somehow catch or kill the bad guy, a dishonest type like some people you know. But no one knows how or why he became a criminal. Often the movies treat criminals like scum, human garbage that has to be removed. It's as if they don't have dreams, don't cry or love."

The audience applauded, and I was surprised at their reaction. The criminals were beginning to identify with the scenario. Perhaps it was the first time they'd had the opportunity to look inside themselves and draw conclusions. Romeo, forgetting the script, was rooting for the bad guy, shouting, "Give it to him good!"

The Mayor and Bartholomew, because of their compulsive speech syndrome, continued to throw in dialogue that wasn't in the script. Clotilde, or rather Bartholomew, couldn't help himself. He put aside the fashion magazine, got up from his armchair, and went to Romeo.

"Sweetheart, my great frustrated politician. Just look at that awful man beating his wife. As a great leader, how can you condone such violence?"

Actually, Bartholomew was playing dirty, trying to incite the Mayor. And he did. The Mayor forgot his character and, assuming the role of protector of women, declared:

"As one of the leaders of this great nation, I proclaim that anyone who strikes a woman, even with a flower, is unworthy of being a man."

"You're the best man in the world," Clotilde said, extending her hand, but then slapping him so hard it sent Romeo reeling.

"What's going on, Honeymouth?" the Mayor raged. He

raised his fists, ready for battle. But Clotilde, batting her eye-lashes, said:

"Sweetheart! Not even with a flower!"

The Mayor bit his lips, held his breath, and saw that Honey-mouth was using the theater to square accounts. Still a bit dizzy from the slap, he looked at the audience, then at his "wife," and tried to maintain the pose of a man:

"Clo, dearest, you nearly sent me down for the count!"

Suddenly, another character ad-libbed. Jurema, playing the granny role, moved behind Romeo while he was arguing with Clotilde and gave him a swift kick in the pants. He jumped to face Granny.

"Get your butt out of that chair and do some work, you bum!"

Clotilde showered her with praise. "You're the best mom in the world."

"Thank you, dear. Oh, the zipper in the back of your dress is open, let me fix it for you."

"Of course, 'Momma,'" said Bartholomew naïvely.

When Clotilde turned around, Jurema gave her an even swifter boot to the backside. Honeymouth dashed away, look-ing back.

"Are you crazy, woman?"

Professor Jurema had been waiting a long time for her chance to settle accounts.

"I'm just beginning, you scoundrel—I mean, hussy," Ju-rema said.

"Nice one, Granny," Romeo said.

You can imagine how the audience of criminals reacted when they saw the two brain-eating theorists of the flatus taking a beating from an old lady. El Diablo, a scowling, ill-humored man who only smiled sarcastically, had never had so much fun. He was like a child.

"Give it to him, Granny," El Diablo yelled. "You deserve it, you drunk!"

Drunk? How did he know Bartholomew had been an alcoholic? Just a lucky guess, I supposed.

I had never been as happy as this in the last few months, finally being able to settle my debts with those two. The dreamseller must have been thinking: What are these people doing? Where are the lessons I taught them?

Heads cooled down, and the characters returned to following the script, at least for a while. Clotilde's mother went back to her sewing. Romeo concentrated on his TV and Clotilde on her fashion magazine. I gave a sigh of relief and returned to the narration.

"Suddenly, when everything seemed calm with this dysfunctional family, a threatening character entered their living room and sent everything off balance. Who was it?" Everyone pondered the question. "A brain-eater," yelled an older murderer who had served thirty-five years.

"Worse than that, sir," I replied. "A mouse!"

At first they were disappointed. They didn't know that Bartholomew was deathly afraid of mice, or that I had to replace the plush battery-powered toy mouse with a small plush bunny so that he, in the role of Clotilde, wouldn't have a panic attack.

But I didn't make the replacement. And still worse, the mouse in my pocket was not battery-powered—it was the real thing. My desire for revenge rose to the surface. I remembered the many times he had called me Superego and said that intellectuals were naïve imbeciles. This then was the moment to settle a few accounts of my own.

CHAPTER 33

The Greatest Crisis in History

THE MEN WATCHING OUR SHOW WOULD SOON LEARN HOW small acts can have rippling effects. They would see that earthquakes are born of small shifts in tectonic plates, a mountain is formed by minute grains of sand, and an ocean by tiny drops of water. The same thing happens in the human brain.

When no one was looking, I let the real mouse loose.

Clotilde's, or rather Bartholomew's, reaction to the tiny animal was dramatic. He screamed so loud he almost gave the Mayor a coronary. He went into a trance for thirty seconds, not knowing whether he was inside a prison or an earthquake.

Jurema, seeing the mouse was real, gasped. She, too, was terrified of rats. I started fanning her with one hand while grasping the microphone in the other to continue the narration. The audience was startled at Clotilde's panic, realizing that things were getting out of control. She was standing on top of a chair, screaming like mad, "Kill it, Mayor! Kill it!"

Unfazed, I continued to narrate.

"Then, inside Romeo's house, the movies came to life—in widescreen and in color. That man hadn't so much as killed a fly in years. Nevertheless he took off his shoe and threw it at the mouse, but he missed. Enraged, he took off his other shoe, aimed at the monster and missed again. He grabbed Clotilde's sandal and threw it as hard as he could at the mouse, which scampered from one side to the other. And he missed.

"Of course he missed, gentlemen! That mouse had a better quality of life than Romeo, who would plop down in his easy chair, do nothing but complain, and never exercise, while the mouse was running around all day long," I said, continuing to narrate the play.

Clotilde, seeing that the Mayor had terrible aim and trying to encourage him to keep after her enemy, threw gasoline on the fire of his feelings of impotence and anxiety. "Are you a man or a mouse? Even a tiny animal gets the better of you!"

"Ten years ago Clotilde and Romeo got married and promised to love each other in sickness and in health, for richer or for poorer," I said to the audience. "But now something as small as a mouse was causing a war in their home." I recalled my own broken marriage and improvised. "We don't trip over tall mountains but over small stones."

Bartholomew forgot he was playing the role of Clotilde and the Mayor forgot he was playing Romeo. Both were mixing their fictitious personalities with real life. Angry at being called a mouse, the Mayor grabbed Clotilde's magazine—"Not the magazine, Romeo!" she yelled—and threw it at the animal, but he missed again.

Romeo began snorting with rage. And despite his enormous weight, he leaped into the air trying to land on the mouse, emitting horrible grunts like an ape-man.

Suddenly, the mouse leaped off the stage and headed toward the audience. And something incredible occurred. Some of those brutes actually climbed onto their chairs. They weren't afraid of facing the police or the army, but they shook like leaves when confronted with a tiny rodent. The mouse set into motion the monsters lurking in the cellars of their minds. After two minutes, a prisoner with the scowling look of a hit man caught the mouse by the tail and returned it to the stage.

Back onstage, the mouse was more cunning than ever, scurrying from side to side. "Come over here, Mickey, come to Daddy Disney," the Mayor said, wishing he could stick the rodent in the microwave as a former mother-in-law had done to him. But the tiny animal outmaneuvered the Mayor and emerged behind him, as if laughing at his aggressor. Then, suddenly, the mouse ran up the back of the Mayor's pants. That wasn't in the script.

The Mayor let out a scream every bit as blood-curdling as Clotilde's: "Eee! Not there, little guy!"

He began shaking his butt, trying to dislodge the intruder. But the mouse scaled the heights with incredible tenacity. Unable to put an end to the wretched creature by himself, he asked the help of none other than Jurema.

"Granny, give this psychopath a good kick."

That was all Jurema needed to hear. She would help out her friend and at the same time get the privilege of once more planting her foot on the street politician's rear. As she paused for thirty seconds to line up the target, the Mayor lost his patience.

"Do it, old woman! He's in the western hemisphere. Careful . . ." As he tried to give away the enemy's position, he shook as if being tickled.

With total concentration, Professor Jurema approached the penalty-shot line, closed her right eye and, at the last moment, backed away, unsure. "Lower that gigantic rump of yours a little."

The Mayor had never been so vulnerable and humiliated, but he obeyed. Jurema took aim again, and this time . . . pow!

The Mayor howled, "Owww! What's the matter with you, old woman?"

"Did I get it?" Jurema asked anxiously.

"Nooooo! You couldn't hit the broad side of a barn, Granny."

Young John Vitor was laughing so hard behind the scenes it hurt. He experienced what crack, cocaine and hallucinogens had never given him.

Seeing Romeo rubbing himself and quivering from the misplaced kick, a prisoner inquired, "But where'd the mouse go?"

Romeo couldn't talk. The animal had invaded his modesty.

"Did he cross the street?" Clotilde ventured to ask her "husband."

The Mayor, almost in tears, confirmed, "Yes! He went to— to the other side," he said impatiently.

I was gasping for breath from laughing so hard. Then the "great politician" implored the elderly Jurema: "Try another kick, Granny. But carefully. Take good aim and let the little devil have it."

Professor Jurema was more than happy to oblige. But in order to avoid another out-of-bounds kick, the Mayor tried to describe the invader's location with pinpoint accuracy.

"He's on top of Sugar Loaf, the right side, two inches from the tunnel."

No way to go wrong, he thought. But Jurema wasn't much for navigation. Once again she requested, "Lower that fat posterior of yours more," causing him to shiver.

Reluctantly, the Mayor lowered his hindquarters. Because the mouse was in constant motion, he started contorting his body like someone on a dance floor. Jurema wanted to do the right thing but didn't know whether to laugh or cry. She looked downward, saw a bulge in the area of the Mayor's right pocket, concentrated, got ready and launched a vigorous kick.

"Owww! You're trying to kill me, Granny," he complained, not knowing whether the target had been hit.

And he reluctantly moved his hand to the spot where Jurema's kick had landed. He stuck his hand into the pocket and protested solemnly:

"You attacked my cheese sandwich, Granny." He took out the sandwich, whose cheese had been smashed from the impact. Instead of continuing the war, he paused, raised the sandwich to his nose, sniffed it as if he were a rat, found the smell reasonably acceptable, and stuck it in his mouth.

The Mayor suspected the mouse had climbed Sugar Loaf because it wanted his sandwich, but he wasn't about to hand it over. As he ate, he philosophized, "Every man needs a cease-fire from his battles. I'm not made of iron. Permit me a pause to eat," he said, chewing with pleasure.

Noticing the mouse moving at will about the Mayor's buttocks, Jurema said, "Now I see why you're so unhappy."

"Quiet, Granny," he said, trying to feel where the mouse was going. The animal had entered his undershorts; the unforeseeable, the unimaginable had unfortunately happened. The Mayor screamed,"Nooooo!"

No one understood anything. Prisoners and guards alike asked in unison, "Where is it?"

Clotilde, trying to pique the Mayor, said, "It's going into the tunnel, Romeo."

The Mayor, crying, turned to her and asked in distress, "How do you know?"

"Female intuition!"

The Mayor jumped around, howling.

"Not there, you little beast! Not there, you killer! You devil!"

The audience was nearly faint from laughing. El Diablo, remembering the theory of the flatus, yelled a recommendation: "Let out a psychopathic flatus."

In a state of shock, the Mayor said, "I'm trying, man. But the car's flooded, the tailpipe's clogged. Your suggestion has failed."

The dreamseller was reveling in watching his loony followers. The comical relationship between Bartholomew and Barnabas was a sociological and philosophical case not found in any textbook.

CHAPTER 34

The Greatest Squeeze in History

AFTER BEING INSULTED BY CLOTILDE, THE MAYOR FOUND HIM-
self in a dilemma. He didn't know whether to punch her out
or flop onto his butt, thus finally crushing his tiny tormentor. He
opted for the latter. It was an act of courage, of valor.

He leaped almost a foot and a half in the air—not much,
but enough to nearly kill himself. That was when the Mayor
experienced the greatest squeeze in history. The suffering was
too much for any man to bear.

When his buttocks collided violently with the floor, he thought
he would never get up again. He was weak and demoralized.

He needed Clotilde, Granny and me to help him to his feet.
Both sides of the Mayor's rear end ached badly. But at least he
felt he had exterminated his enemy, as it had ceased moving
about. When he examined his posterior, however, his expression changed; he turned white, purple, then red. Something
terrible had happened.

The mouse was still alive. And it set off rapidly on an extremely dangerous course. So dangerous that this time the
Mayor did a somersault without falling.

"Not there, you little creep!" he shouted. "Oh, God, don't go
there, you skunk!"

No one understood a thing. "Clotilde bit her lip and asked, 'Did he, um, take the subway?'"

Almost sobbing, the Mayor confirmed: "Yes!"

"Subway?" we asked, confused. Seconds later, seeing his distress, we decoded his language. The mouse had snuck through space between his legs and onto the other side, the forbidden area.

Biting his lips, the Mayor said, in an almost inaudible voice, "Get away from there, you shameless little bastard! Oh, oh! He's playing basketball."

My friends, the theater rolled with breathless laughter. Psychopaths who had never let their guards down laughed like school children.

But that wasn't the worst of it for the Mayor. "He's climbing my Statue of Liberty!" he yelled.

Words fail me to describe the two combatants. The Mayor was like mythological fire-breathing dragon and the mouse was mocking him. That was when I realized my trap had exceeded my expectations. I pitied him. I felt he had paid for all the sins he had committed against me and the rest of the group—with interest. I wanted to help him. But how? Unfortunately, he had to suffer martyrdom alone.

As the dreamseller told us, "There are times when we are alone, profoundly alone, in the midst of the multitude. At such times, neither expect nor demand anything from anyone. You must stand by yourself." The Mayor was profoundly alone, in the middle of more than a hundred people who wanted to help him but couldn't. The prisoners wanted to rescue him; the guards, dying of laughter, wanted to set aside their weapons and offer moral support. Smiles and comedy had united criminals and policemen.

There was another option—to take off his pants and search

for the mouse in the cellars of his intimacy in that lair of men. But an experienced politician would never reveal his "sins" in front of others; it would be the end of his career, he thought. So he stuck with the alternative.

He would solve the problem on his own. A good swift blow at the correct angle and his enemy was a goner. But he was panting, and the immediate environs of the target were delicate. He might never have children if he missed. He held his breath, raised his right hand, took aim—and then Granny spoke, destroying his concentration.

"Leave it to me, my son. This time I'll get him." And she approached, ready to launch a kick.

"No! Not here, Granny. If you miss, a lifetime of Viagra wouldn't cure me. This is a job for a professional," he said with conviction.

He covered his eyes with his left hand, raised his right hand into the air like a general commanding his last battle, and prepared to strike. Everyone watching, including me, instinctively protected our own groins. Pitilessly, the Mayor pummeled himself.

The blow was so powerful that we all groaned in unison, as if experiencing the same pain.

"Aaaaaaaaiiiiiiiiii!"

The Mayor was literally paralyzed. We didn't know if he was dead or alive. We held a minute of silence out of respect for his bravery. After that dramatic period when you could hear a pin drop, we all asked:

"Did you kill it? Did you kill it?" The Mayor didn't answer. The pain was so great that he couldn't form an utterance.

"Did you kill it?" we insisted. After two long minutes, he spoke, haltingly and slurring his words.

"I crushed my *bolitas*. I'm sterile. Oh, oh!" Unfortunately, the fleet-footed mouse had managed to escape the final battle and win the war. Great politicians, especially the shrewdest ones, are destroyed by tiny pests. Politicians create the rats and the rats corrupt the politicians.

He would have to leave the stage and drop his pants, totally humiliated, beaten, shattered. As if the humiliation and pain weren't enough, Clotilde added to his wounded pride: "No problem, Romeo, you haven't been up to it for a long time now."

Enraged and unrecognizable, the Mayor moved toward Bartholomew. But as he took the first steps, the mouse abandoned the Statue of Liberty, took the subway, went down Sugar Loaf, and slowly descended the Mayor's leg. When it reached the floor, it was staggering, dizzy, stunned.

"The Mayor's slap had no effect, gentlemen, but his primitive scream was the winning blow. He inflicted a mortal wound on the poor animal," I said.

They all watched the sluggish motions of the mouse. They liked him, as did I. The jaunty little animal moved uncertainly, listing first to the right, then to the left. Stopping then advancing with slow steps. Two yards further on, it raised its right paw, placed it on the left side of its chest, looked at the audience like some brilliant actor, and succumbed. It lay on the floor, its paws upward. It had suffered a heart attack.

"The poor thing kicked the bucket," said Honeymouth, who in all the confusion had overcome his phobia about rats and tamed that ghost. "For the first time, I fell in love with a rat."

"The mouse died of stress," I explained to the crowd. "Be careful that you do not suffer the same fate."

It was then that the greatest criminals in the country discovered they were dying like the mouse, through stress and anxiety. Because they were not productive, constructive, creative or contemplative in their cells, they lived tense, embittered, stressful lives. Ten criminals had already suffered heart attacks on Demons Island that year, twenty had cancer, and the majority had other stress-induced conditions. Which confirmed the idea that, imprisoned or free, human beings inhabited a huge madhouse.

The dreamseller always warned us that out in the global mental hospital in which we all lived, few of us free men and women had ever committed crimes against others. But we never failed to commit crimes against ourselves. I was one of those criminals, more machine than man, working and studying, irritable and impatient. I was incarcerated in my own private prison, although the professors and students of my university believed I was free. It was all an illusion.

Clotilde, seeing her enemy motionless on the carpet, rose from her chair, looked at Romeo and said affectionately, "Dear Romeo, you're my hero."

Romeo, feeling like the good guy in the film, the most fearless of men, inflated his chest, raised his voice, and declared his love.

"Clotilde! For you I flattened my basketballs, sacrificed the Statue of Liberty and leveled the Sugar Loaf. Thanks to that miserable rat, I'm not the same man anymore."

And they shared a Hollywood kiss.

Both had placed a small apple between their teeth and pretended they were kissing. Provocatively, Clotilde jumped into the arms of Romeo, who fell and choked on the apple. He had to be clapped on the back to expel the fruit. The Mayor, though lightheaded, still had the spirit to say, "Clotilde, the rat killed me . . . and you buried me."

At the end of the play, they both went to the center of the stage along with Professor Jurema. And even before they took a bow, these criminals—feared by judges, prosecutors, and the FBI—rose to their feet and gave them a standing ovation.

"The moral of the story," I said, after the applause had died down, "is that Clotilde and Romeo live happily ever after until—" And the prisoners responded as one:

"Another mouse comes into the picture!"

CHAPTER 35

Cellars of the Mind

THE INMATES BEGAN TO UNDERSTAND THAT RATS ON THE outside may die, but those scurrying around inside the secret spaces of our minds reproduce over time. They can't be exterminated, only tamed. They began to understand that it did no good to destroy external foes when their real enemies were inside them. It was a fantastic lesson.

I whistled, the mouse awoke, came running toward me, and I scooped it up. Everyone was astonished. That's when everyone discovered I had hired a trained mouse. He was a great actor. Everyone applauded for the tiny animal. Including Honeymouth. The Mayor put his hands on his head and whispered, "Vote for me, you little bugger, and I'll forgive you for all this humiliation."

I turned to the audience and asked, "Have we forgotten any characters?"

Everyone looked toward the stage and saw two actors with their hair standing up. Yes, we had forgotten to clap for the "children."

At that moment, I asked the dreamseller to come up to the stage. He protested, but I insisted. It wasn't planned, but those men with shattered histories needed to hear him as I had.

He agreed. The criminals had a hard time believing that a

homeless beggar could be the leader of the group. The dream-seller ran his eyes over the audience, waiting to start in.

He didn't want to give a lot of explanations, so he once again chose the Socratic method.

"Can a small mouse be transformed into a monster? Can a small stone become a wall in our minds?" Then he asked them to search their histories and try to find small issues that had been transformed into great conflicts.

Twenty people raised their hands. "Shotgun," a stone-cold killer, stood up in the second row and began telling his story.

"Every time I urinate I give a little jump. The reason is that when I was a child, a Doberman bit me at the exact moment I was urinating. From then on, I couldn't go without jumping," he said, laughing.

I was taken with his boldness. I would never have guessed that these men harbored such subtle thoughts. The dreamseller continued.

"In the play, the children registered both the image of the mouse and the image of their parents' reaction. The im-ages merged in their unconscious, becoming one and the same thing. That process increased the destructive power and the threat of that small animal. The mouse became a real monster, a ghost, a trauma."

The stage lights dimmed, soft music began to play. And, demonstrating that life is cyclical, that there is time to smile and time to cry, he urged those present to be wanderers in search of themselves.

"Travel within your story. Remember the tears that were dammed up inside you but were never seen on your cheeks. How many losses and acts of violence suffocated you when you were boys? How many hugs were denied? How many de-privations did you suffer? Many of you had your childhoods crushed when you should have been playing like children."

The inmates journeyed to the past and were moved. El Diablo and Shrapnel were puzzled by the dreamseller's generosity. The latter in particular had accused and threatened the dreamseller. He had offered them a shoulder to cry on as he helped them dissect their pasts. Terrorists, murderers, drug dealers and thieves were left defenseless by all they had just seen and heard. It was now the moment for them to go below the surface and penetrate into the deeper layers of their minds.

"Think now, without fear, of the childhood you destroyed, the lives you shattered and the dreams you crushed. So many traumas! So much anguish you caused! So many irreparable losses you brought about! There are many things that explain your traumas and your suffering, but none of them justifies inflicting suffering on others," he said without fear of retribution.

"Violence explains violence," he said, "but no act of violence justifies violence."

Hearing him, I remembered the professionals who had died there in the last two years during riots. I also remembered that Fernando Lataro and other prison workers were marked for death. And I recalled how my students had been run off the island without succeeding in interviewing even the least dangerous prisoners. Now, here—face to face—the dreamseller was speaking to the leaders of the penitentiary about their most grievous mistakes, and they were listening without resentment in their hearts.

Then he addressed one of the best known texts in history, and one of the least understood. He spoke of the ghosts of betrayal, denial, and guilt.

"At the Last Supper, Christ was deeply saddened by his disciples. The most intelligent of them, Judas Iscariot, would betray him, and the strongest, Peter, would deny him. Which of these crimes is the greater?"

I had never thought of those two famous historical mistakes from the standpoint of sociology. Where was the dreamseller heading?

"Both were extremely grave betrayals. Judas betrayed him once, Peter denied him three times, vehemently. But the lessons Jesus taught us are powerful. He did not punish his betrayer. Just the opposite; he broke bread with him, showing in a veiled manner that he had no fear of being betrayed. In this way, he revealed to us that our errors must be rectified with the nourishment of education, symbolized by the bread. Nor did Christ condemn his denier, Peter. He shouted silently to him: I understand! He gave Judas and Peter the tools to tame the ghost of guilt and thus gave them the chance to start over. Only Peter made use of them. Judas was torn apart by his demons. Will you be?"

The dreamseller pressed them further.

"Are you guilty? Yes. Whoever fears recognizing his mistakes will take the ghosts that haunted his mind to his grave. Face your ghosts and you will have some chance of taming them.

"More than eighty percent of you—the majority under forty years of age—will grow old in prison and rot in this place. Many others will leave here hunched over with age. And about half of you will only leave the island in a body bag, sentenced to life in prison. I know that every day, when you think about your hair turning white, your muscles losing their strength, and your eyesight failing in this cold and gloomy prison, you go into a state of panic. Can you tame those ghosts and survive with dignity? That's the biggest question. A crime takes place in minutes, but its consequences can last a lifetime."

And, in an inspired moment, the dreamseller breathed deeply and continued.

"I also committed crimes, but not those found in the criminal statutes. I have debts to my conscience that I know I'll never be able to repay." Hearing the leader of the group, without coat and tie, dressed worse than they, confess to unpayable debts reached them in the depths of their souls. None had ever opened the pages of his story in that maximum security prison.

At that exact moment, El Diablo whispered something to Shrapnel and other leaders of a faction who were sitting beside him. The dreamseller stripped himself bare before those fragmented men.

"My crime? Today I'm homeless. But, like some of you, I loved money more than people. Dollars were my god. I was a child in the theater of time and never marveled at the phenomenon of existence. I was dead even as I lived. I had never made an inventory of my life.

"I never spoke to my children about my tears so they could learn to cry theirs, never spoke to them about my fears so they could face theirs, never spoke about my mistakes so they could learn to overcome theirs. By the time I realized I should do things differently—when I dreamed of hugging them, asking their forgiveness, of leaving my mental prison—time betrayed me. My two children died in an airplane crash in the rainforest."

The dreamseller caught his breath.

"Who can settle that debt for me? What law? What prison? What psychiatrist? What friends? What amount of money? I'm to blame and can't hide from it. Every day, I have to tame the ghosts that point out my insanity and prevent me from starting over. I'm not looking for understanding, sympathy or reprieve. I'm looking to find myself. I'm a wanderer. There is no oasis in my desert. I must create one in order to survive and remake myself."

Then he asked the inmates to reflect on two important moments—one in which they had been injured and another in which they had injured someone else—and to make bridges between them. He wanted them to search for the only freedom that cannot be imprisoned behind iron bars. The only one that, if lost, can transform existence into the most unbearable of dungeons.

CHAPTER 36

Ripping the Soul

ITTLE BY LITTLE, MORE THAN TWO THIRDS OF THE IN-
mates, men who had never had the courage to talk about
themselves or listen to the misfortunes of another, crumbled.
They knew what crimes they had committed and the laws
under which they had been punished. They knew the weapons
they had used. But not the losses they had suffered or the tears
they had shed.

Some confessed that when they took drugs for the first time
they swore they'd never use them again. But then came the second time. And the third. Others talked about the first time they
stole, how they vowed never to do it again. But then came the
second time. And the third. Still others confessed they'd had
insomnia for many nights the first they shot a person. But other
crimes soon followed, finally annihilating their conscience.

Some of the criminals in the theater were weeping as they
spoke of the wounds they had suffered or caused. They were
irreparable errors. Lives had been lost, children had been injured. In making a brief inventory of their stories, they lac-
erated their mental core and seemed to return to the womb
in search of protection. After twenty minutes, we left quietly,
without saying good-bye. They were still talking about their
monsters, unrestrained, fearless.

As we left, Fernando Lataro and some of the staff, social workers and psychologists were beaming. They couldn't thank us enough. The warden felt that everything he had seen and heard had helped not only the inmates, but him, too. Seeing his enthusiasm, the dreamseller threw cold water on him.

"Everything that happened today is just a drop in the sea of their needs. No one changes anyone. There is no magic to overcoming conflicts. Memory isn't wiped out. No one leaves the hell of his mistakes unless he finds the door to paradise: compassion and education.

"Maybe there could be classes in theater," the dreamseller, added. "Maybe Demons Island could have elementary education. Trades and courses in technology could be taught via satellite. Maybe there could be music and art classes. Maybe there could be computers with access to limited areas of the Internet for their distraction and to expand their minds instead of allowing them to think about foolishness and feeding their ghosts and permitting their unchecked desire to flee."

Fernando Lataro gave a rather ironic smile. "Dreamseller, we have no money. The prisoners are treated like human beings in theory, but in practice they're treated worse than society's garbage."

One of the staff members added, "Even the federal government has abandoned the island."

"No business would ever invest a cent in this human sewer," a psychologist said.

The reality was raw, cruel and painful. Everything would go back to what it was in that factory of criminality. We had ideals but no money. The only one with resources was Professor Jurema, who had assets but no income. The dreamseller took Dimas aside, looked him in the eye, placed both hands on his shoulders, and almost inaudibly, gave him an order that made us laugh like crazy.

"Dimas, see to the resources."

"Dimas, go rob the Central Bank," Bartholomew said, laughing.

"You're looking at the next guest of Demons Island," said the Mayor, then apologized to the dreamseller. But since he too was laughing, we thought he was satirizing the financial crisis.

If even the two loonies thought the dreamseller's order was a joke, imagine how the rest of us felt.

"No need to protect your pockets, folks," Edson said. "We're all poor." And he broke into laughter along with the rest of us, including Fernando Lataro.

"Master, Dimas is going to need Edson to pull off the miracle of the loaves and fishes," I added.

"Look at that. The intellectual has a sense of humor, after all. Congratulations!" Honeymouth said.

I had seen Dimas hoodwink a lawyer who had just gotten him out of jail after a petty theft because he didn't have a penny on him. Dimas and the dreamseller were in the same boat. But, to our amazement, Dimas innocently thought the dreamseller was speaking in earnest. Like the chancellor to a king, he asked jubilantly, stuttering as always, "Are you sp-sp-speaking seriously?"

"Yes, Dimas, perform the miracle without Edson," said the Master, smiling.

Dimas hummed and danced like a child. He hugged the Master, kissed him on the cheek, and grabbed his right hand, raised it overhead and danced with him.

The team almost burst a seam laughing. Philosophy had taken on a sense of humor never seen before. The warden and his subordinates didn't take the dreamseller's proposal seriously. After all, dreams and delirium are close relatives.

Two days later, we were walking down a busy street when suddenly the wind blew a page from a big-city newspaper into my face. As I was about to put it in the trash, a headline caught my eye: "Mellon Lincoln Jr. may be alive."

"It can't be," I thought. Mellon Lincoln Jr. had been expected to be the presidential candidate of one of the major political parties. But since death doesn't discriminate, it had come knocking at his door. When he died, I was living in Russia, separated from my wife and far from John Marcus.

I was out of the country for a year, doing my postdoctoral, and knew no details about that powerful leader's misfortunes. He was such a celebrity that I thought the article about Mellon Lincoln was just another sensationalist effort to increase circulation.

The dreamseller was also an unrelenting critic of the man. I remembered that the first time we went to Jurema's house he made very unflattering comments about him.

I quickly handed the paper to the dreamseller. His expression changed. "They want to bring back the dead," he said, shaking his head. "Society stupidly looks to its past heroes. It doesn't invest in the revolution of the anonymous."

CHAPTER 37

Banning and Wounding the Man in Rags

I T WAS THREE IN THE AFTERNOON ON A WEDNESDAY. THE dreamseller had given us some pears and apples he had received from an admirer. We hadn't had lunch and were famished. While we ate the fruit, I glanced sideways and saw the dreamseller eating a near-rotten pear. It was always that way: he gave us the best he had.

As our hunger wasn't satisfied, we stopped in front of a fancy French restaurant to ask for any leftover food. I told the group, "This isn't our kind of place."

"O, ye of little faith. Let's give it a try, brother!" Edson replied.

Elegantly dressed people leaving the restaurant eyed us and gasped. The Mayor made a gesture indicating he was feeling faint from lack of food. And he was. If he went more than two hours without chewing on something, he would get dizzy. Fruit barely moved the needle.

The owner saw the rabble in front of his fine establishment and quickly directed us to the area in back, where he would serve us. We were pleased at the prospect of eating dishes from that famous restaurant. On a professor's salary I would have had to work for a week to spend an hour there.

Frowning, the owner appeared with two security guards

and placed the food on disposable plates. After serving the dreamseller, he became aggressive, animal-like. He spat into his food and ordered, "Don't ever come back unless you want to go to jail."

As the owner turned to enter the restaurant, the dreamseller pushed aside the part where the owner had spat, and told him, "Thank you, Jean-Pierre, for your kindness. The *rôti* sauce is delicious."

The restaurant owner's eyes widened, he started to pant, his voice caught in his throat. Like the director of Mellon Lincoln Hospital, he reacted as if he'd seen a ghost. Once again we didn't understand the significance of these events.

The next day, after a two-hour walk from the bridge where we slept, we came to an enormous building, forty stories high with a mirrored exterior, surrounded by a magnificent garden of tulips, multicolored daisies, and chrysanthemums: the headquarters of the powerful Megasoft group.

The dreamseller crouched down to observe a tulip. He asked us to breathe in its perfume and contemplate its anatomy. Immediately, a guard came to shoo us away. We were on the sidewalk, a public place. However, the guard didn't back down.

We were hungry again but decided to give French cuisine a wide berth. Monica had some change that at most would pay for her lunch. Professor Jurema had forgotten her purse. Crusher was broke. John Vitor barely had enough for a grilled ham and cheese sandwich.

We would sing, the dreamseller would recite poetry and give speeches and people would spontaneously donate whatever they felt like giving. That was our major source of income. We didn't ask for alms, we weren't professional beggars. We were poor by choice. The dreamseller never had us ask for money, and only rarely did we ask for leftovers at restaurants. But his disciples were always breaking the rules.

Four well dressed men who appeared to be Megasoft executives passed us on their way to the main building. The Mayor, overcome with hunger, asked them for change. "Most esteemed men of commerce. Could you finance lunch for this future leader of the nation and his advisers?" he said, pointing to us.

"Get out of here, you bum," the most senior among them said.

The Mayor scaled down his request: "A few coins will do."

To get rid of him, the guy took two dimes out of his pocket, and instead of placing them in the Mayor's hand, arrogantly threw them onto the sidewalk.

"These beggars ought to be sent off to Iraq," he said as he walked away.

The dreamseller was overcome with indignation.

"I remember a young man who in a speech as head of a corporation said: 'A great executive must value the human being more than the product he manufactures.'" He paused, then added, "But time belies speeches."

The businessman stopped and took a step back, startled. His eyes widened and, astonished, he asked, "Who are you?"

"That doesn't matter. What matters is, who are you?"

The dreamseller ran his eyes over the magnificent building that housed the Megasoft group and nodded. Then he spotted a lovely tree a few yards away and improvised a poem that disturbed the "gods" in ties and touched my very soul:

More generous than men are the trees that extend their
    arms to travelers,
inviting them to rest in their shade.
Once they have rested, they turn their back and leave
    without a goodbye.
The trees neither complain nor ask for anything in return.

*More giving than men are the trees, which house the birds
     that flock to their branches.*
*The next day, they depart without paying rent or offering
     thanks.*
*But the trees say farewell by applauding with the
     movement of their leaves at the touch of a breeze.*
They give of themselves with pleasure.

The four executives stood rooted to the spot, unable to explain the sensation overtaking them. Their legs wouldn't move. They were silent, speechless. Without another word, the dreamseller bent down, picked up the two coins and returned them. "What's not given freely offers no relief."

One of the executives, a man with white hair, apologized, but the man who had thrown the coins couldn't react. He had to be led away by the arm.

And as they left, the dreamseller applied the coup de grâce. They wouldn't sleep for nights on end.

"When I fall dead on the streets and you lie in a grand mausoleum, it will be the same thing. We will all be equal in our smallness."

Afterward, instead of leaving the scene, the dreamseller made an unusual decision. He decided to enter the headquarters of the Megasoft corporation.

Just then, we were blocked by three security guards. We were barred without even being asked our identity, based solely on our appearance. Appearances open doors, but it's intelligence that defines the journey. Doors never opened spontaneously for us.

"Leave immediately or we'll call the cops," they said, pushing us away.

"This is the legacy of Mellon Lincoln Jr., the billionaire who created the culture that expels people," the dreamseller said, finally losing his patience. "A sick legacy, exclusionary and elitist. Go ahead and call the 'gods' of this institution. I want to speak to them."

Other Megasoft executives passing by took offense at the criticisms of their great founder. The dreamseller had shaken the dogma of their religion, the temple of finance. He had attacked an untouchable guru. One of them looked at us from head to toe and said, "What asylum did this band of psychos break out of?"

We didn't exactly blend in. The dreamseller was wearing patched black pants and a white shirt with an ink stain in the pocket. I was wearing a white polo shirt and blue jeans. Solomon had on green denim pants and a yellow T-shirt. Bartholomew and Barnabas looked like something from another planet. Except for the two women, Jurema and Monica, we stood out for all the wrong reasons."

"No one is worthy of being a leader of business if he's not first a leader in the theater of the mind. And no one will be a leader in the theater of the mind unless he learns to see beyond the outward trappings," the dreamseller said, unnerving the young executives.

"Who's this beggar who memorizes sayings from philosophers and recites them to impress us?" one of them asked.

No one knew. Then they ordered their security officers, "What are you waiting for? Toss these buffoons out of here."

"We come in peace," Honeymouth said. And he told the Mayor, "Send in the heavy artillery."

"You mean," Barnabas asked, "the killer flatus?"

And the Mayor let loose a deadly burst of gas.

The executives beat a hasty retreat. On their way up in the elevator they contacted security, claiming that a band of terrorists were in the lobby. This caused a stampede. Immediately,

two dozen guards carrying a wide variety of weapons, including AK-47 assault rifles, stormed the building, holding us at
gunpoint.

They quickly overpowered us. They violently threw the
dreamseller, Bartholomew, Barnabas and Solomon to the floor.
The rest of us froze where we were. They searched us, humiliated us, insulted us. After determining that the dreamseller
was the leader of the group, a guard put his foot on his neck
and mercilessly twisted his right arm. He was being suffocated.

He shouted demands for the dreamseller to identify himself,
but our leader remained silent. They fruitlessly looked for iden-
tification. They actually believed he was a terrorist disguised
as a ragamuffin.

They lifted him up from the floor. Because one of the
guards had pressed his foot against the dreamseller's trachea,
he coughed violently. One of the guards slapped him in the face
to make him stop faking. That violence was unimaginable in
a democratic society. Being branded a terrorist is worse than
being a leper. They are killed first and identified later.

Recovering from his coughing fit, the dreamseller still had
enough breath to strike the only way he could.

"Who pays your salary?" he asked.

"None of your business," said the head of security.

"Does Mellon Lincoln or his estate pay your salary for you
to be polite or aggressive, to prevent or to punish?"

The security chief punched him in the stomach and then
in the face. He dropped him to the floor and stuck his pistol in
the dreamseller's mouth, injuring his lips and teeth. The docile
dreamseller was bleeding. The women cried and called the relentless guards murderers.

Bartholomew tried to come to his aid but took a blow to the
chest and was knocked flat.

"What do you know about Mellon Lincoln?" the chief of security shouted. Taking the gun from the dreamseller's mouth, he bellowed, "Who are you? Identify yourself!"

The dreamseller was uncooperative.

"The ruthless billionaire who only cared about making money infused his cold inhumanity into this firm. Is this brutality his policy?"

The security chief pistol whipped the dreamseller on the head, tearing a gash into his scalp. Blood began to run down the dreamseller's face, creating a horrifying image even worse than the week before, when he had been attacked near Luiz Lemos's house.

This man of peace was attacked ruthlessly. We were all staring down the barrels of guns, unable to help him. Indifferent to the dreamseller's wounds, the security chief, who undoubtedly had killed people in the course of his profession, pressed the gun against his neck and yelled, "You're Al-Qaeda, aren't you?"

The revolver had become a god that could decide life or death. In the past, Mellon Lincoln Jr. had suffered a terrorist attack, after which his group, already concerned about his safety, had become paranoid. All of the company executives had bodyguards.

Watching this scene play out made me think about the dreamseller's criticism of the social system. And humans belonged to the system. Without a "reputation," it wasn't possible to exist or survive in our society. Rousseau would have to modify his motto: man is born with his instincts, and society educates or imprisons him. If the dreamseller continued to insist on his unusual way of life, it would soon cost him his life. The sociological experiment that had attracted me would end in disaster. Human beings had become their own predators.

Despite his dizziness and his bleeding, the dreamseller managed to turn his head slightly and face his aggressor. "Humberto," he said, "without mankind and its welfare as its focus, Megasoft practices its own form of terrorism."

The security chief's hands went limp, barely able to hold the revolver.

"How do you know my name?"

I looked to see if the security chief wore a name tag, but he didn't. Humberto repeated the question but was drowned out by the sound of ten police vehicles. Thirty heavily armed policemen swarmed in, handcuffed the supposed terrorists, and took us away like criminals to be interrogated. No one cared about the dreamseller's wounds. Hundreds of people approached. Some of them knew the dreamseller. They looked at his forehead and cheek covered with blood and became outraged at the cruelty with which he had been treated. They began to protest, shouting. But no one listened to them. Several journalists photographed him handcuffed. As we were about to get into the paddy wagon, the chief of police showed up. He approached the group and went straight to the dreamseller.

"You again?" he said, grimacing as he saw the dreamseller's bleeding wounds. "I've been following your work. And I fear for your life. Get out of this city and keep quiet, for your own good."

"If I keep quiet, the system wins," the dreamseller said.

"You can't change things. You have to see that," the police chief said.

"I'm a sower of ideas. My responsibility is to bury those seeds."

And the police chief just shook his head, knowing there was no silencing him. He told the guards to let us go, saying that he knew us, had already questioned us and that we represented no danger.

"You see, people? We beat the police. No one can shut us up," the Mayor said enthusiastically.

"Quiet, Mayor," said Monica.

The police chief wanted to take us to an emergency room to treat the dreamseller's cuts and bruises, but he refused. Several people wanted to hug him but kept their distance because of his hands, which were bloodied from wiping his face. Despite that, more than a few said, "Thank you very much for your words. You've changed our thinking." And they immediately dispersed.

Professor Jurema came forward, gave him her handkerchief, and told him, "My son, I'm proud of you. It's an honor to follow you."

"But it's not safe," the dreamseller said. "All of you must leave."

We knew he was right. But we looked at each other and knew we couldn't abandon him. An indescribable force united us. Staying near him was as dangerous as a desert and as refreshing as a mountain spring.

CHAPTER 38

The Pain of Slander

THE NEXT DAY'S HEADLINES WERE SENSATIONAL. SOME defended the dreamseller, saying that a prejudiced society doesn't tolerate people who are different. They stated that a gentle and intellectual man had been wronged. Another denounced him as a dangerous man. I had a fit of rage when I saw that headline. Honeymouth crumpled up the newspaper, and the Mayor started to chew it. But the dreamseller was calm and told them softly, "We are what we are. The dimension of our conviction about who we are determines the level of our protection or our vulnerability."

But nothing infuriated me as much as when I saw his picture with blood running down his face on the front page of the city's leading newspaper, which the Megasoft group owned. The headline read: "Seller of nightmares attacks again." And it stated that the dreamseller consorted with prostitutes, bums and alcoholics—in a word, the worst strain of society. People should avoid contact with him; the young should ignore him. The article went on to say that the great social phenomenon could be one of the biggest psychopaths the city had ever seen.

Even the dreamseller seemed disappointed. The newspaper had interviewed only one party in the story, namely the Megasoft executives who suspected he was a terrorist and the security guards who had abused him at the corporate head-quarters.

The article added that he was an atheist who believed only in himself. He wanted to be a kind of Christ, a god in his own century. Without ever investigating him, they had thrown his inventory in the trash. The newspaper coverage influenced some. One person who read the article slapped the dreamseller and spat in his face. "You want to be Christ? You're an atheist, a man not worth his own life," the stranger told him

Wiping his face, the dreamseller looked his aggressor in the eye and said poetically and serenely, "Yes, I was an athe-ist among atheists. To me, God was the fruit of a diminished mind, a superstitious and reductive mind. But, though I defend no religion, when I analyzed the 'son of man,' and his ability to shape generous human beings even when he was betrayed and seen as social trash, I saw my own childishness. And you who follow him, do you recognize your childishness before him?"

The man went away speechless.

As a sociologist, I pointed out to my students that a jour-nalist who doesn't investigate both sides of a story equally is a disgrace to his profession. It was almost unbelievable that the newspaper had been so partial.

The story led to a biased and totally slanderous view. It pro-claimed loudly on page one that the homeless man nicknamed the dreamseller has caused an uproar at the stadium, had at-tacked the director of Mellon Lincoln Hospital and incited a riot on Demons Island, slandered the founders of the Mega-soft group and had instigated an unprovoked assault on that group's security guards.

The article tried to destroy him as critical thinker. It called him a scoundrel, a fraud, an impostor, a con man. He was vi-olent, vengeful, and possibly a psychopath, it said. It recom-mended that people stay away from him.

I looked at the dreamseller and saw him saddened. The gentlest and wisest man I knew had been thrown into society's trash bin. Even worse, he had no way to defend himself. They might as well convict him in the court of public opinion and sentence him to Demons Island.

And speaking of that island, the same newspaper did run a story that filled us with joy. Two theater groups were beginning to function full-time in the institution. Music and art teachers had been hired. In addition, Demons Island was to receive a hundred computers. Word came to us unofficially that at last money from the government would be forthcoming.

We were happy for Demons Island but anguished over the slanders in the newspaper. I remembered what the dreamseller had said. He valued journalistic criticism but considered prejudice a cancer to society.

"Criticism acknowledges existence, while prejudice annuls it," he said. "In the land of the blind, a one-eyed man is a stranger, the object of scorn and rejection."

After reading the story, we began walking down one of the city's best-known streets. My friends and I were melancholy. A man who looked to be around seventy, wearing a dark suit, white shirt, and a striped yellow tie, rapidly came toward us. As he got within ten yards, he flashed an unforgettable smile. He spread his arms and with uncontained joy ran to greet the dreamseller. It was an encounter overflowing with jubilation. But we didn't understand a thing. Perhaps it was someone who admired him but didn't know him.

The stranger embraced him affectionately, talking nonstop.

"You're alive! I can't believe it!"

To our surprise, the dreamseller responded with tears in his eyes. One of the wounds from the beating of the night before had opened and begun to bleed.

"Forgive me, I've gotten blood on you," the dreamseller

started to say. But the man demonstrated that not only was he intelligent but a gentleman as well.

"It's an honor to be stained by the blood of the man I love and admire the most," the stranger said.

The dreamseller put his hands on the other man's shoulders and nodded in gratitude.

Then he greeted us all. But he greeted Dimas with more feeling and joked, "How's the kleptomania? Have you overcome it?"

"Still the joker," the dreamseller said.

I didn't understand anything. Ever since I began accompanying the dreamseller and started writing this manual of dreams, I've become more confused. The consolation is that ideas are born in the terrain of discomfort.

The stranger was astonished at the dreamseller's battered appearance. "Good Lord, you're injured! What did they do to you? Tell me, which hotel are you staying in?"

Bartholomew broke out laughing.

"The best hotels in the city: overpasses, bridges, park benches and homeless shelters."

"What? You're sleeping under bridges? At least stay at one of your hotels."

"My dear man, you're speaking to the wrong person. The dreamseller is as poor as a church mouse," said the Mayor.

All of us were closely following that unusual conversation. The dreamseller answered the stranger, ignoring the Mayor. "I rest in the bed of peace and make the stars my blanket. You don't know the sheer joy of being a simple human being."

"But you could get sick. You look destroyed! What restaurant have you been eating at?"

"At Mr. Gutemberg's bakery. Day-old bread and lots of leftovers," Edson said.

"What? No, I can't believe it! You used to eat in the best

restaurants. It was your favorite luxury. What restaurant do you want me to buy?"

The tenor of the conversation staggered me. We had to humiliate ourselves anytime we wanted to eat. We had to jump through hoops, sing, put on clown acts and depend on the kindness of others to eat. Now this man came along proposing to buy the dreamseller a restaurant? Honeymouth couldn't hold his tongue any longer.

"Hey, I know all about food. I'll pick the restaurant," Honeymouth said.

The man speaking to the dreamseller looked at the band of misfits who followed him, and found them odd company. And he had just met us. Imagine if he spent a day with us!

"You can't deny who you are!" he said emphatically.

The dreamseller gave a soft, ironic laugh and replied, "Who am I? Today I look at myself and I'm astounded to confirm that I only knew the superficial levels of my being."

"You can't deny your past. You were the greatest businessman of the last decade and became one of the richest men on earth, even with the stock market crisis."

"Rich, me? What riches can bring back what I love the most? What amount of money can buy the source of happiness, the fountain of hope and the wellspring of dreams? If you accuse me of being rich, I admit it: yes, I'm rich. I have what money can't buy."

He paused, and pointed to us.

"Look at my friends; they're my treasure. They love me for who I am. They love a ragged man, a man without glamour, status, money, a pauper. Yes, I'm rich. I have eyes to see the flowers, I have time for the things without names. I have the smiles of children to nourish me, the experience of the elderly to instruct me in serenity, and the madness of psychotics to make me see my own insanity. Yes, I'm rich. I have what's important.

I have what neither gold nor silver can buy. What about you? Do you have those things?"

The stranger stood there silently and gave a wan smile. He realized that the dreamseller still possessed a brilliant sense of reasoning, better even than the last time they'd seen each other.

"I can't say that I do," he said. But he didn't give up. "I'm not speaking of those solemn riches, Master," said the elderly man, calling him Master for the first time. "I'm talking about that which men covet."

"Did you know that money attracts enemies and drives away true friends?"

"Yes, I do know. It's the system."

Honeymouth, the street philosopher, affirmed, "Money is like a corpse that feeds bacteria and attracts hyenas." Then he again patted himself on the back: "Gee, what brain cell did I extract that from?"

"If you lose everything you have, even your children and your image in society, how many people will stand by you?" the dreamseller told the man.

After a warm silence, the stranger answered, "Maybe far fewer than I dare believe. But you can't deny your power. It extends to every continent. Kings admire you. Celebrities fade in your presence. Presidents court you."

"Power? What power do I have, Charles?" the dreamseller said, using his friend's name for the first time. "Every day I die a little. Every day trillions of cells that make up my fragile body need to be nourished to keep from collapsing. Every day time howls in my mind reminding me that life, however serious it is, is only a play in eternity. Every day, time shouts at me that soon I'll perform my final act. What power do I have, Charles? Tell me."

"Wake up, man!" said Bartholomew. "We're the poorest people in the city. Can't you see that?"

"Dear Mr. Charles, do you maybe have some spare change you can lend me?" the Mayor asked.

The stranger scrutinized the pair of compulsive talkers from top to bottom and minced no words.

"I don't think your disciples are kaleidoscopic."

The Mayor drew close to Honeymouth and whispered, "Did that guy just praise us or insult us?"

"Good question," he said.

"But I like the word," the Mayor said.

"Don't you think your followers should be a team of intellectuals?" Charles told him.

"Intellectuals? In the Master's school, intellectuals and crazies are on the same level," Honeymouth said. "What you need is experience!" And he looked at me provocatively. But I was pensive and deeply interested in the conversation between the dreamseller and the stranger.

The dreamseller looked the man in the eye.

"If you knew my followers, you'd discover they are coarse, honest, ingenuous—different from us," he said. "Their wisdom doesn't come from the academic world, their sensitivity isn't revealed in art exhibitions, their fame isn't made known by the media. They live in anonymity, away from the spotlight, as if they were without merit. But I guarantee they are fascinating human beings."

After this praise, Bartholomew and Barnabas went around greeting all the disciples, congratulating them on being fascinating.

"I pity Hollywood, pity TV, pity magazines that ignore us," said Honeymouth proudly, striking an actor's pose.

"Yes, we are the great ignorant ones," the Mayor said, and I just shook my head.

CHAPTER 39

The Great Revelation

THE STRANGER DIDN'T KNOW WHAT TO SAY. HE WAS SPEECH-less in the face of the bizarre group that followed the dreamseller. The dreamseller saw we were confused and felt he should give us some information about his past. Instead of denying that he had been courted by kings and celebrities, he said, "Forget who I was. What matters is who I am."

Hearing this, I almost collapsed. If he was telling us to forget who he was, it was confirming that he was someone great. It wasn't possible to rationalize that information. It didn't fit into any logical framework.

My mind swarmed with questions. If the dreamseller had been so extremely rich in the past, how did he end up with almost nothing? He was a generous homeless person who divided what he had with those who had nothing. He would give up eating to feed the hungriest.

Not even the most rabid socialists dispensed with the privileges of comfort. Some of them, like Stalin, Brezhnev, Ceaușescu, and Kim Jong-Il, loved luxury more than capitalists did, even when their people went hungry. Marx wrote about the government of the proletariat, but not even he relinquished his comforts.

In Nietzsche's terms, the dreamseller was human, all too

human. It was impossible to imagine that he had abandoned everything. Yes, he denounced a social system that had become a factory for producing sick people. Yes, he desired to sell the dream of a free mind. But not because he was a spiritual prophet or a messiah, but because he was a prophet of philosophy. He denounced the barbarity of modern society because he had developed critical thinking.

But if he were rich, how could he disdain the privileges of his work and his success? Only if he was unbalanced, crazy, unhinged. But none of that matched the facts. His intelligence exposed my own stupidity, his wisdom dissected my madness, his maturity revealed my childishness.

I could only conclude that the stranger was just flat wrong. He was just one more admirer who exalted him as a social hero for trying to change the way of society. This dreamseller, who even frequently took the subway to save money for food, couldn't have been admired by kings.

While I was pondering these questions, the dreamseller replied to the elderly, serene man who begged him to give up his life as a homeless wanderer.

"I don't have a blanket to sleep under, but I have the mantle of tranquillity. I don't have money to throw extravagant parties, but I celebrate life every day. I'm penniless, but I own everything that enchants my eyes. I have nothing to buy, but I sell dreams."

Charles was motionless, paralyzed. The dreamseller always confused those who heard him. But his friend made one last effort.

"If you want to sell dreams, you at least need to treat your injuries. Go to the hospital that you established in honor of your father," Charles told him.

I flushed and gasped for breath. After recovering, I blurted out: "What hospital?"

The stranger was silent for a moment. He looked at the dreamseller and received his approval to speak.

"Mellon Lincoln."

"What? Mellon Lincoln? I can't believe it! That can't be right!" I said, almost speechless. "Then you're . . . Mellon Lincoln Jr. The powerful head of Megasoft! The man slated to lead this country."

The dreamseller said nothing, and I was dumbfounded. All my friends also stood mute—even the compulsive talkers. I stared at the dreamseller's bruised face and pulled out the newspaper with the old photo of the handsome Mellon Lincoln Jr. I compared them, and my blood froze.

The dreamseller could see it in my eyes. I couldn't think. From beneath the rubble of my thoughts, I stared at the man who had rescued me from jumping off the top of the San Pablo Building.

"I criticized you several times in the classroom. I thought you were despotic, cold, removed from the plight of society, alienated from human conflicts," I said. "But look at you now, a pauper, a pauper who became my master. I heard you tear into Mellon Lincoln Jr. several times. I heard you provoke the executives of the Megasoft group, denouncing the founder of the institution—you yourself. Why? Why, for God's sake?" I asked, stupefied and using the word "God," something I, an atheist in transformation, rarely did.

The dreamseller sighed deeply. A crucial moment in our relationship had arrived. He looked at each one of us.

"Are you astonished? The *Homo sapiens* incapable of criticizing his sapience is unworthy of being *sapiens*. How could I survive without destroying my mind? How could I rescue my lucidity without denouncing my acts of insanity? How could I move on without recognizing my austerity, my damages and my stupidity?"

CHAPTER 40

The Creature Devoured by Its Creator

ALL MY FRIENDS WERE AS PERPLEXED AS CHARLES—EXCEPT for Dimas, that is. We had branded him a con man and a swindler, but to our surprise he was the young assistant to Mellon Lincoln Jr.

Dimas suffered from kleptomania and a complicated past. As a kleptomaniac, when an object, often without monetary value, entered his field of vision it set off a mental trigger that aroused a compulsion to possess it.

As an adolescent, he had robbed Mellon Lincoln Jr., whose bodyguards had caught him in the act. Instead of punishing him, Mellon Lincoln Jr. protected and educated him. He paid for his studies and made him into a kind of secretary to his family. We found out later that the dreamseller's children loved him. But Dimas broke down after the children's death and the dreamseller's mental collapse. But we still didn't have all the details about this relationship. Jurema seemed to have a gut feeling about his identity, but I had thought she was senile. Now I believe she had just preferred to keep quiet.

Bartholomew, Barnabas, Edson, Solomon, Monica, Crusher and several others who followed the dreamseller were trying to digest all this new information. They couldn't believe he had given up his comfortable life, scorned his power and turned his back on his status and fame. They replayed the last few months in their minds and were more confused than ever. They launched a battery of rapid questions at him.

"Master," said Monica, "you were humiliated at the stadium by leaders of the worldwide chain of ladies' clothing La Femme, a subsidiary of your company. And you let it happen! Why?"

"You were blocked from the entrance of your corporation as if you were some criminal," Edson added.

"And you were beaten by security guards whose salary you pay," Bartholomew, said, adding, "That's it, I'm gonna take those guys down . . ."

"You were slandered, called a lunatic and even a psychopath by the newspaper that's owned by your Megasoft group," Solomon said, dumbfounded.

"And you were almost killed by lethal injections in your own hospital!" I reminded him, indignant.

The dreamseller raised his eyes and saw some sparrows chirping and dancing in the air. Breathing deeply, he returned his gaze to his group of friends.

"The creator carefully raised his creature only to have it grow and bare its teeth against its master. An animal that needs to be whipped to be tamed will never be your friend, will never let you sleep in peace," he said, deeply upset. He then added, "If the Megasoft group turned against its creator, imagine what it does to strangers."

"Well I don't have to imagine. I *know*. The friends you trusted have become vultures," Charles said angrily. "The men who injured you don't know you."

"You think they really don't know me? Perhaps those who injured me don't know my identity, but some of those who want to take my life know quite well."

"I'm at your service, Mr. Lincoln," Charles said. "Who are

these enemies of yours? Who do you want me to punish? Who should I fire or send to prison?" Heads would roll.

Before the Master could respond, Bartholomew and the Mayor had already made a list of the heads that should be severed.

"That no-good who runs the hospital. Send him to Iraq for a year. Two journalists, five security guards, four executives. Let's see, who else . . . Ah! Tulio de Campos, who never liked Julio Cesar."

But the dreamseller cut them off emphatically: "For now, no one is to be punished!"

"No one?" the Mayor replied, dissatisfied. "It's our grand chance to wipe out these bastards!"

Charles, also indignant, said, "What do you mean, no one? They almost killed you. They're not worthy of walking around free, much less working for your company!"

"There are no saints in this story. I was to blame for instilling a philosophy that crushes the humanitarianism of those I led. The lack of money impoverishes us, but its misuse makes us miserable," he said.

Hearing him, I thought, "I don't have his maturity and dignity. If it were up to me, heads would roll. I used to cut students and professors off at the knees in the sociology department I ran for much less."

The dreamseller was a billionaire who lived under bridges. He was enriched by that which can't be bought. Then he repeated what he had told El Diablo on Demons Island.

"Besides, Charles, the greatest revenge against an enemy is—" And before the dreamseller could finish the phrase, Charles completed it:

"I know, I know. It's to forgive him . . . Just like your father used to say. He died because of it, as you well know."

I realized that Charles had known the dreamseller inti-
mately since childhood. And so he was naturally extremely
concerned about the dreamseller's living conditions and about
the premeditated attempt on his life at the hospital.

"Either you assume your power or you must leave the country and sell your ideas somewhere they can't find you. Maybe
in one of your summer homes in the Greek isles, in Scandinavia
or French Polynesia."

"My bags are packed!" the Mayor said.

I couldn't believe my ears. As a university professor I suffered to pay the mortgage on my small, modest house, and the
Master had several summer homes he never used. What kind
of self-denial was that? "I don't have any bags to pack," the
dreamseller said, joking with the Mayor. He turned to answer
Charles.

"I almost died of guilt, depression and anguish in one of
those summer homes. Today, I say let each day bring its own
problems and its own solutions. Maybe the homeless man will
work things out and find a reason to be what he once was.
Maybe the pauper speaking to you will one day find joy in assuming his miserable throne of gold."

Charles had admired Mellon Lincoln Jr. long before he had
faced his demons, before losing his children. He knew him to
be courageous and bold, with a rare creative spirit and an un-
shakable determination. Charles understood that no one could
convince him to change his path, once he had made up his
mind. "I promised your father on his deathbed that I would
never abandon you. If you need me, you know where to find
me. Oh, and that siren that scared away the five men who almost killed you wasn't just a stroke of luck. I tried to do what I
could to protect you. An informant I had tail you said you still
know how to handle yourself with martial arts, but we still
haven't had any luck finding out who hired those assassins."

Charles sighed deeply and put his hands on the dream-seller's shoulders before leaving. "Mellon . . . son, you're very important to a lot of people, but you're putting your life at risk. Please be careful." He took out his wallet and tried to give him over a thousand dollars, but the dreamseller refused. With tears in his eyes, Charles left silently.

Bartholomew and the rest of us bit our fingers, wanting to grab the dough. The dreamseller had twenty bodyguards, five armored cars, two private jets, but he had preferred freedom, with all its dangers, to being kept in a dungeon illuminated only by the light of society's spotlight. Incomprehensible? Yes, the man we followed had a complex mind. And he tried to ex-plain himself.

"If I had a thousand years to live, maybe I would go back and spend time on what I consider secondary. But because our time on earth, from childhood to old age, disappears in an in-stant, I can't afford the luxury of living without freedom. I don't ask you to understand this, only to respect it."

CHAPTER 41

Great Men Also Weep

W E NOW KNEW WHO THE DREAMSELLER WAS AND WE were all stupefied. He had gone out into the world seeking to confront the conflicts that haunted him. He had been part of the very system he criticized. Now, it was time to be free.

He looked again at the swallows flying overhead and recited the wanderer's anthem, hoping his words would take flight and be as free as the birds.

"Who am I? Powerful? Famous? No! I'm just a wanderer who lost the fear of getting lost. You may call me crazy, you may mock my ideas. It doesn't matter. What matters is that I'm a wanderer who has learned to break out of the cell of routine."

An hour later, we found ourselves back in the courtyard of the federal courthouse. We were flying high, for now we felt we were following a powerful man. That made us ecstatic. Everything would be simpler, we thought. Our paths would be smoother, our days more at ease, our existence infused with more creature comforts. We should have known better.

A man with grayish hair, who looked to be around fifty, came quickly up to me and placed an envelope in my hands, then left without identifying himself. It was addressed care of the old friends Honeymouth and the Mayor and signed by none other than El Diablo.

I was startled at first. It was only then that I discovered my two companions had been longtime friends with the infamous Demons Island leaders. I handed the letter to them, and they glanced at each other before opening it. Bartholomew took the initiative and gave me a quick explanation.

"El Diablo and Shrapnel were friends of ours from the orphanage. We were lost to drinking and they were lost to a life of crime."

They opened the letter and began reading it together. I moved away to respect their privacy. As they read, their lips started to tremble for the first time. A sudden anguish overcame them. They were paralyzed. They dropped to their knees, tears covering their faces.

I had never seen those two jokers who always made light of even the most serious things, fall to pieces. But they did. They lost all their joy, their good spirits. Of course, I wanted to know what was in the letter. They handed it to me, nearly drained of all strength. It had been addressed to them but in reality it was intended for the dreamseller. I began reading the short letter and was as astonished as Bartholomew and Barnabas. I couldn't believe what I was reading. The dreamseller's enemies had beaten and slandered him and now they intended to bury him.

The last thing in the world I wanted was to hand that letter to the dreamseller. Everyone else wanted to read it, but I couldn't bring myself to show it to them. Short of breath, flushed, I walked tensely toward him. He saw my emotional state and, I instantly saw the tension build on his face.

The dreamseller took the letter. As soon as he read the opening lines, for the first time since we'd known him, we saw him break down. He was no longer the invincible, intrepid leader we had followed. Instead, he transformed and became a disturbed, shaken man.

After finishing the letter, he fell to his knees as Bartholomew and Barnabas had done. His heart had been ripped out mercilessly. He raised his hands to the heavens and shouted:

"Noooo! It can't be!" He screamed the names of his two children, Fernando and Julieta, over and over. He clenched his eyes closed and wept bitter tears.

Everyone in the square froze. It was as if the dreamseller were dying. And he was—inside. Expressing inexpressible pain, he began to sob and say repeatedly, "No! No! Because of me—no!"

The letter fell from his hands and the wind blew it to Professor Jurema. She caught it and read it to the other members of the group.

To the seller of dreams,

I was touched by your words on this miserable island, and I felt I should give you a piece of news— even though I know hearing this will be the worst nightmare of your life. You said the best revenge against an enemy is to forgive him. And now, I am asking for yours. I know that every man has his limits, especially where his children are concerned. You should know that two of your closest "friends" at Megasoft paid to hire a hit man. Your children didn't die in an accident. Everybody thought you would be on board flight JM 4477 on March 23. You were the target.

Signed,
El Diablo

The disciples stood silently in that immense courtyard. There were no birds singing, no caress of the breeze, no rustling leaves. A few passersby chuckled at seeing a man on his knees, weeping. That's the human story. Some are depressed while others smile, some shout while others remain silent.

We wanted to console the dreamseller, take him in our arms, say anything that might soften his pain, but it was impossible. His anguish was so deep that no words could lessen the blow.

In light of this information, a great dilemma would mark the dreamseller's story. As he had told us, enemies can frustrate, but only friends can truly betray us. The dreamseller has two false friends who committed the ultimate betrayal, men more violent and powerful than any criminal on Demons Island. Men who had probably dined, walked and laughed with the dreamseller but who sank to the lowest depths of crime. Who were these psychopaths? Why did they commit that unspeakable act? What would the dreamseller do? Would he continue to be homeless? Would he take up his seat as one of the most powerful men in the world? Would he run in fear of his pursuers or plot his revenge against those who killed his children? Consumed with hate, would he renounce his belief that violence does not justify violence? Would he be able to see the difference between vengeance and justice? Would he stop selling dreams and distill hatred instead?

And what would he do with us? We had built an altruistic unprecedented brotherhood. Given the risks he'll face from now on, would he abandon us? Would we be able to live apart from one another? Some of us might get by. I have my university, Jurema has her possessions, Solomon his house, Monica her apartment, Edson his religion. But what about Bartholomew and Barnabas? They have nothing. They're street wanderers with no address or protection. All they have is the dreamseller and their new family. They knelt and both wept for the dreamseller's children. They had adopted him as their father, a ragged father who didn't punish, exclude or shame

them, one who embraced them, loved them and invested everything he had in them. There was a completely unselfish, poetic,
serene and unexplainable love between them.

I remembered something the dreamseller had said: "You're
responsible for the consequences of your choices."

Every man has to make choices. The moment had come
for him to make his greatest choice. Would he continue to
explore his path or would he be afraid of losing himself?
Would he go back to the cult of celebrity, of which he had
been so critical?

Dozens of questions hurtled into my mind. And I didn't
have any answers. I only knew that he had managed to reorganize his fragmented history in masterly fashion, but now his
being had again been shattered into a thousand pieces. I had
seen him go off alone, night after night, talking to his children
in his imagination, begging their forgiveness for the time he
didn't spend with them, for trying to give them the world but
denying them his presence—which is all that really mattered.

This intriguing man taught us that the greatest test of all
was taming our ghosts. But now the ghosts of anger, pain, revenge and retaliation emerged like a sudden earthquake to
haunt him. Would he pass the greatest test of all?

As a philosophical thinker, he had solemnly defended the
thesis that existence is cyclical. Drama and comedy, tears and
joy, peace and anxiety are privileges of the living and inexora-
bly alternate for every human being.

What would he say now? Would he abandon his own belief?
How would he deal with the cycle of existence? I didn't know.
I only knew he would have to go from the seller of dreams to
buyer of dreams. He would need the most intelligent and lucid
to bear the full consequences of his own theory: "Life is like a
theatrical production, the show of shows. When we close the

curtain on the theater of time, the show doesn't end; the spectacle continues for the audience in tears."

At that moment I saw him on his knees, spent, simply a part of the sobbing audience.

Great men also weep, and when they fall, they shed inconsolable tears . . .

THE END

(of the second volume)